# William Shakespeare's Much Ado About Nothing: A Retelling in Prose

David Bruce

Published by David Bruce, 2022.

WILLIAM SHAKESPEARE'S MUCH ADO ABOUT NOTHING: A RETELLING IN PROSE

**First edition. July 27, 2022.**

Copyright © 2022 David Bruce.

ISBN: 979-8201672089

Written by David Bruce.

# Table of Contents

# Dedication

**Dedicated to Carl Eugene Bruce and Josephine Saturday Bruce**

My father, Carl Eugene Bruce, died on 24 October 2013. He used to work for Ohio Power, and at one time, his job was to shut off the electricity of people who had not paid their bills. He sometimes would find a home with an impoverished mother and some children. Instead of shutting off their electricity, he would tell the mother that she needed to pay her bill or soon her electricity would be shut off. He would write on a form that no one was home when he stopped by because if no one was home he did not have to shut off their electricity.

The best good deed that anyone ever did for my father occurred after a storm that knocked down many power lines. He and other linemen worked long hours and got wet and cold. Their feet were freezing because water got into their boots and soaked their socks. Fortunately, a kind woman gave my father and the other linemen dry socks to wear.

My mother, Josephine Saturday Bruce, died on 14 June 2003. She used to work at a store that sold clothing. One day, an impoverished mother with a baby clothed in rags walked into the store and started shoplifting in an interesting way: The mother took the rags off her baby and dressed the infant in new clothing. My mother knew that this mother could not afford to buy the clothing, but she helped the mother dress her baby and then she watched as the mother walked out of the store without paying.

***

The doing of good deeds is important. As a free person, you can choose to live your life as a good person or as a bad person. To be a good person, do good deeds. To be a bad person, do bad deeds. If you do good deeds, you will become good. If you do bad deeds, you will become bad. To become the person you want to be, act as if you already are that kind of person. Each of us chooses what kind of person we will become. To become a good person, do the things a good person does. To become a bad person, do the things a bad person does. The opportunity to take action to become the kind of person you want to be is yours.

Human beings have free will. According to the Babylonian Niddah 16b, whenever a baby is to be conceived, the Lailah (angel in charge of contraception) takes the drop of semen that will result in the conception and asks God, "Sovereign of the Universe, what is going to be the fate of this drop? Will it develop into a robust or into a weak person? An intelligent or a stupid person? A wealthy or a poor person?" The Lailah asks all these questions, but it does not ask, "Will it develop into a righteous or a wicked person?" The answer to that question lies in the decisions to be freely made by the human being that is the result of the conception.

A Buddhist monk visiting a class wrote this on the chalkboard: "EVERYONE WANTS TO SAVE THE WORLD, BUT NO ONE WANTS TO HELP MOM DO THE DISHES." The students laughed, but the monk then said, "Statistically, it's highly unlikely that any of you will ever have the opportunity to run into a burning orphanage and rescue an infant. But, in the smallest gesture of kindness — a warm smile, holding the door for the person behind you, shoveling the driveway of the elderly person next door — you have committed an act of immeasurable profundity, because to each of us, our life is our universe."

In her book titled *I Have Chosen to Stay and Fight*, comedian Margaret Cho writes, "I believe that we get complimentary snack-size portions of the afterlife, and we all receive them in a different way." For Ms. Cho, many of her snack-size portions of the afterlife come in hip hop music. Other people get different snack-size portions of the afterlife, and we all must be on the lookout for them when they come our way. And perhaps doing good deeds and experiencing good deeds are snack-size portions of the afterlife.

The Zen master Gisan was taking a bath. The water was too hot, so he asked a student to add some cold water to the bath. The student brought a bucket of cold water, added some cold water to the bath, and then threw the rest of the water on a rocky path. Gisan scolded the student: "Everything can be used. Why did you waste the rest of the water by pouring it on the path? There are some plants nearby which could have used the water. What right do you have to waste even a drop of water?" The student became enlightened and changed his name to Tekisui, which means "Drop of Water."

Educate Yourself

Read Like A Wolf Eats

Be Excellent to Each Other

Books Then, Books Now, Books Forever

***

In this retelling, as in all my retellings, I have tried to make the work of literature accessible to modern readers who may lack some of the knowledge about mythology, religion, and history that the literary work's contemporary audience had.

Do you know a language other than English? If you do, I give you permission to translate this book, copyright your translation, publish or self-publish it, and keep all the royalties for yourself. (Do give me credit, of course, for the original retelling.)

I would like to see my retellings of classic literature used in schools, so I give permission to the country of Finland (and all other countries) to give copies of this book to all students forever. I also give permission to the state of Texas (and all other states) to give copies of this book to all students forever. I also give permission to all teachers to give copies of this book to all students forever.

Teachers need not actually teach my retellings. Teachers are welcome to give students copies of my eBooks as background material. For example, if they are teaching Homer's *Iliad* and *Odyssey*, teachers are welcome to give students copies of my *Virgil's* Aeneid: *A Retelling in Prose* and tell students, "Here's another ancient epic you may want to read in your spare time."

# CAST OF CHARACTERS

**Male Characters**

DON PEDRO, Prince of Arragon.

DON JOHN, his bastard Brother.

CLAUDIO, a young Lord of Florence.

BENEDICK, a young Lord of Padua.

LEONATO, Governor of Messina.

ANTONIO, his Brother.

BALTHAZAR, Servant to Don Pedro.

BORACHIO, CONRADE, followers of Don John.

DOGBERRY, a Constable.

VERGES, a Headborough.

FRIAR FRANCIS.

A Sexton.

A Boy.

**Female Characters**

HERO, Daughter to Leonato.

BEATRICE, Niece to Leonato.

MARGARET, URSULA, Waiting-gentlewomen attending on Hero.

**Minor Characters**

Messengers, Watch, Attendants, etc.

***Nota Bene***

The title *Much Ado About Nothing* contains wordplay. A thing is what a man has between his legs. A woman has no thing between her legs, so the title can be interpreted as *Much Ado About Pussy*. Given that this play is a romantic comedy, that title is correct.

In addition, in Elizabethan England "nothing" and "noting" were pronounced the same way. In the play, a lot of noting occurs — people note what other people say and do. Frequently, they misinterpret what they note, and this leads to complications in the play.

# CHAPTER 1

## — 1.1 —

Standing in the garden in front of the house of Leonato, the Governor of Messina, were Leonato himself, his daughter, whose name was Hero, and his niece, whose name was Beatrice. Also present was a messenger sent to Leonato by Don Pedro, the Prince of Aragon. The messenger had just given Leonato a letter about a battle fought between the forces of Don Pedro and his illegitimate half-brother, Don John. Don Pedro's soldiers had won the battle, and afterward, Don Pedro and Don John were reconciled.

"I learn in this letter that Don Pedro of Aragon is coming tonight to Messina," Leonato said.

The messenger replied, "By this time, he is very near. When I left him, he was not nine miles away from Messina."

"He has just fought a battle," Leonato said. "How many gentlemen — men of the upper classes — did he lose in the battle?"

"Few of any rank," the messenger replied, "and none of any great importance."

"A victory is won twice when the victor brings home alive nearly all of his soldiers," Leonato said. "I read in this letter that Don Pedro has bestowed much honor on a young Florentine named Claudio."

"Claudio much deserved the honor, and Don Pedro has properly rewarded him for his actions in the battle. Claudio performed deeds in battle that no one would expect such a young man to do. Despite having the figure of a lamb, he performed the feats of a lion. Claudio indeed exceeded all expectations of him so much that I cannot tell you all that he did."

"Claudio has an uncle here in Messina who will be very happy to hear of his heroism."

"I have already carried to Claudio's uncle letters that made him very happy," the messenger said. "The uncle felt so much joy that he broke out in emblems of what sometimes expresses bitterness."

"Did he break out into tears?" Leonato asked.

"In great measure. He cried much."

"That was a kind overflow of kindness as expressed by kindred. No faces are truer than those that are so washed by tears. How much better it is to weep at joy than to joy at weeping! It is much better to cry with happiness than to rejoice at someone's unhappiness."

Beatrice asked, "Please tell me whether Signior Mountanto has returned from the wars or not."

Beatrice thought, *The messenger will not understand my joke, but Hero will. I am referring to Benedick. A montanto is an upward thrust in fencing — it starts low and goes upward — and a stallion mounts a mare. Benedick is a ladies' man, and he and I have a history.*

The messenger replied, "I know none of that name, lady. No one of any rank in the army bears that name."

"Who is he whom you are asking about, niece?" Leonato asked.

"My cousin means Signior Benedick of Padua," Hero replied for Beatrice.

"Oh," the messenger said. "He has returned, and he is as pleasant and amusing as he ever was."

"Benedick once set up public notices here in Messina to announce that he was challenging Cupid to an archery contest," Beatrice said. "He claimed to be a better lady killer than Cupid. Cupid is blindfolded, but his golden arrows have a great impact when they hit someone — that person instantly falls in love. By claiming to be superior to Cupid in archery, Benedick was claiming that he would never fall in love — and that he would make more women fall in love than Cupid could.

"My uncle's fool, reading Benedick's challenge, responded on behalf of Cupid, and competed against him in the archery contest. My uncle's jester used bird-bolts in the contest — blunt arrows used to stun birds. Bird-bolts are given to children and to fools. My uncle's fool mocked Benedick."

She added, "Please tell me how many soldiers has Benedick killed and eaten in these wars? Better, just tell me how many he has killed. Benedick is a braggart who boasts about his prowess in many kinds of hunting, and so I promised to eat all of his killing. I do not think that he is enough of a soldier to kill anyone."

"Truly, niece," Leonato said, "you criticize Benedick too much, but he will find a way to get even with you, I am sure. Benedick can give as good as he gets."

"Benedick has done good service, lady, in these wars," the messenger said,

"You had stale food, and Benedick has helped to eat it. He is a very hearty eater; he has an excellent stomach."

"He has an excellent stomach for battle," the messenger said. "He is a good soldier, too, lady."

"He is a good soldier compared to a lady, but what is he compared to a lord?" Beatrice asked.

"He is a lord compared to a lord, and a man compared to a man. He is stuffed with all the honorable virtues," the messenger replied.

"You speak truly, indeed," Beatrice said. "Benedick is no less than a stuffed man — he is a dummy — but what is he stuffed with? He is full of — shh, I ought not to finish that sentence. We are all mortal."

"You must not, sir, mistake my niece," Leonato said to the messenger. "Signior Benedick and she wage a kind of merry war. They never meet without engaging in a skirmish of wit between them."

"Benedick performs poorly in those skirmishes," Beatrice said. "People have five wits: memory, fantasy, judgment, imagination, and common sense. In our last skirmish, four of his five wits went limping off, and now the whole man is governed by one wit. If he has enough wit to keep himself warm in cold weather, let him know that it is what differentiates him from his horse. Human beings are the only rational creatures, and Benedick's one wit is what allows him to be known as a reasonable creature."

She added, "Who is his male friend and companion now? He has every month a new sworn brother for life."

"Is that possible? You must be exaggerating," the messenger said.

"No, it is very possible," Beatrice said. "He pledges his faith to each new friend just like he changes the fashion of the hat he wears. With each change in fashion, he wears a new hat."

"I see, lady, that the gentleman is not in your good books — he is not in your favor," the messenger said.

"No, he is not," Beatrice replied. "If he were, I would burn my library. But please tell me who is his new male friend? Is there no young hooligan now who will make a voyage with him to the devil?"

"He is most often in the company of the right noble Claudio."

"Benedick will hang upon Claudio like a disease. Benedick is more contagious than the plague, and the catcher of the Benedick illness becomes immediately insane. God help the noble Claudio! If he has caught the Benedick illness, it will cost him a thousand pounds before he can be cured."

The messenger thought, *This lady really is clever. The Benedictine priests are exorcists and attempt to cure madness. She made a good pun on "Benedick."*

"Lady, I will take pains to always be friends with you and so avoid becoming the victim of your tongue," the messenger said.

"Do so, good friend," Beatrice replied.

"You will never catch the Benedick disease and run insane, niece," Leonato said.

"No, not until there is a hot January in Italy," Beatrice replied.

The messenger heard a noise and looked around. He said, "Don Pedro is coming here now along with some other people."

Don Pedro and Don John, his illegitimate half-brother, with whom he had recently quarreled but then been reconciled, approached, along with Claudio, Benedick, and Balthasar, a singer and attendant who worked for Don Pedro.

Don Pedro said, "Good Signior Leonato, you are meeting your trouble. The fashion of the world is to avoid expense, but by hosting us you are encountering it."

"You are never a trouble to me," Leonato said. "Never came trouble to my house in the likeness of your grace. Trouble being gone, comfort should remain; but when you depart from me, sorrow stays and happiness leaves."

"You embrace the burden of my visit too eagerly," Don Pedro said. He nodded at Hero and said, "I think this is your daughter."

"Her mother has many times told me so," Leonato said.

"Were you in doubt, sir, that you needed to ask her?" Benedick joked.

Leonato joked back, "Signior Benedick, no. I knew that I was the father of my daughter because when she was born you were only a child. If you had been an adult, I might have had my doubts."

"Your joke has been answered, Benedick," Don Pedro said. "All of us know that you are a ladies' man. But truly the lady fathers herself. All we need to do is to look at Hero to know that Leonato is her father. Be happy, lady, because you resemble your honorable father."

Don Pedro and Leonato then went aside and spoke privately.

Benedick joked, "Even if Signior Leonato is her father, she would not want to have his head on her shoulders for all Messina, as like him as she is. Signior Leonato is bearded and has grey hair."

"I wonder that you are always talking, Signior Benedick," Beatrice said. "No one is paying attention to you."

"What, my dear Lady Disdain!" Benedick replied, "Are you still alive? I would have thought that you had died by now."

"It is impossible for Lady Disdain to die while she has such suitable food to feed it as Signior Benedick," Beatrice replied. "Courtesy itself must convert to disdain, if you come within her presence."

"Then courtesy is a traitor," Benedick said. "But it is certain that I am loved by all ladies, with the exception of only you, and I wish that I could find in my heart that I had not a hard heart because, truly, I love no one of the opposite sex."

"That is a precious piece of good fortune to women; otherwise, they would have been troubled with a pernicious and harmful suitor. I thank God and my cold blood that I am like you in loving no one of the opposite sex. In fact, I prefer to hear my dog bark at a crow than to hear a man swear that he loves me."

"May God keep your ladyship always like that!" Benedick said. "That way, some gentleman or other shall escape an otherwise predestined scratched face. Anyone who marries you can expect to be scratched."

"Scratching could not make the gentleman's face worse, if it were a face such as yours."

"You are an excellent parrot-teacher," Benedick said. "You would do well at teaching a parrot because you say the same kind of things over and over."

"My talking bird is better than your dumb beast," Beatrice replied. "A bird can say something, but a beast cannot."

"I wish that my horse had the speed of your tongue, and could gallop as long as you can talk," Benedick said. "But keep on talking — I have finished talking."

"I have known you a long time," Beatrice said. "You are like a jade — an ill-conditioned horse. You always end with a jade's trick — you fade and cannot go the distance."

Having finished their private conversation, Don Pedro said to Leonato, "That is all I have to say," and they rejoined the others.

Don Pedro said, "Signior Claudio and Signior Benedick, my dear friend Leonato has invited both of you to stay with him. I told him that we shall stay here at least a month, and he heartily hopes that some occasion may detain us here longer. I dare to swear that he is no hypocrite, but speaks from his heart."

"If you swear, my lord, you shall not commit perjury," Leonato said.

He then said to Don John, "Let me bid you welcome, my lord. Now that you have been reconciled with the Prince your brother, I owe you all my allegiance."

"I thank you," Don John said. "I am not a man of many words, but I thank you."

Leonato said to Don Pedro, "Will it please your grace to lead everyone into my house?"

"Let me have your hand, Leonato," Don Pedro said. "We will go inside together."

Everyone went inside except for Benedick and Claudio.

"Benedick, did you notice Hero, the daughter of Signior Leonato?"

"I saw her, but I did not take any special notice of her."

"Is she not a modest young lady of good conduct?"

"Are you asking me, as an honest man should, for my real and simple and true judgment?" Benedick asked. "Or are you asking for the answer that I, in my persona of a self-confessed enemy to and critic at every opportunity of the female sex, would give?"

"I am asking you for your real and simple and true judgment. Speak seriously and give me your true opinion."

"Why, I think that she is too low — too short — for a high praise. I think that she is too brown and suntanned for a fair praise of her beauty. I think that she is too little — too small — for a great praise. I can give her only this praise: If she looked different from the way she looks, she would be ugly. Still, because she is a she, I do not like her."

"You think that I am joking," Claudio said. "Please tell me truly whether you like her."

"You are asking a lot of questions about her. Are you thinking of buying her?"

"Can the world buy such a jewel?"

"Yes, and a case to put it into," Benedick said. He smiled, knowing that a case could mean a jewel-box or a suit of clothing. It also meant a sheath, such as a sword fits into. The Latin word *vagina* means sheath, and Benedick knew that if Claudio were to "buy" Hero by marrying her he would gain a sheath to put his "sword" into.

Benedick asked, "Are you asking me these questions seriously? Or are you being a flouting Jack — a scornful fellow — and trying to tell people that Cupid — who is blind — is good at finding hares and that the blacksmith god Vulcan is an excellent carpenter? Are you serious or satiric? I need to know what key you are in before I can sing in harmony with you."

"In my eyes, Hero is the sweetest lady whom I have ever seen," Claudio said.

"I can still see without spectacles, but I cannot see what you see," Benedick replied. "I look at Hero and at Beatrice, who is possessed by an ancient Greek avenging spirit known as a Fury, and I see that Beatrice is more beautiful than Hero just like the first day of a spring May is more beautiful than the last day of a winter December. But I hope that you have no intention of becoming a husband. Are you thinking of marriage?"

"Even if I had sworn never to marry, I do not think that I would keep that promise if Hero were to agree to become my wife."

"Has it come to this?" Benedick complained. "In all the world does not even one man exist who need not wear a cap out of suspicion that his wife has been unfaithful and made him sprout horns to provide evidence to the world that he is a cuckold? Shall I never see a 60-year-old bachelor again? But since you want to be married, go ahead and thrust your neck into a yoke and wear its imprint as you sigh on Sundays because you cannot get away from your wife and enjoy bachelor games."

Benedick looked around and said, "Look, Don Pedro has returned to seek you."

Don Pedro walked up to them and said, "What secret conversation have you been holding here that has kept you from joining us in Leonato's house?"

"I wish that your grace would force me to tell you," Benedick said.

"I order you — who have allegiance to me — to tell me."

"You heard Don Pedro, Count Claudio," Benedick said. "I can keep a secret as well as a man who cannot speak — I hope that you know that — but I have pledged my allegiance to Don Pedro and that outweighs other considerations.

So, Don Pedro, listen well. Claudio is in love. With whom? I am sure that is the next question you would ask me. The answer is short: He is in love with Hero, Leonato's short daughter."

"What Benedick says is correct — assuming it is true," Claudio said.

"This is like an old tale in which a statement is denied, and is denied again, and is finally revealed to be true," Benedick said.

"Unless I change the object of my love very quickly," Claudio said. "I hope that God will forbid me to love someone else."

"Amen, if you love Hero," Don Pedro said, "The lady is very well worthy and ought to be loved."

"You are trying to trick me into admitting that I love her," Claudio said.

"I am saying only what I truly believe," Don Pedro said.

"I also said only what I truly believe," Claudio said.

"By my dual loyalties to you, Don Pedro, and to you, Claudio, I also said only what I truly believe," Benedick said.

Finally, Claudio admitted the truth: "I feel that I love Hero."

Don Pedro replied, "I know that she is worthy of your love."

Benedick said, "In my opinion, I neither feel how Hero should be loved nor know that she is worthy of being loved. That is an opinion that fire cannot melt out of me. If I were to be burned at the stake like a heretic, I would die still holding this opinion."

"You were always an obstinate heretic when it comes to beauty," Don Pedro said. "Courtly love is not a religion you follow."

"You believe what you believe through stubborn determination," Claudio said.

"That a woman conceived me, I thank her, and that she brought me up, I likewise give her most humble thanks," Benedick said. "However, I intend to avoid having a cuckold's horns on my forehead — I want to neither display them openly nor try to hide them. Therefore, women will have to pardon me for not wanting to be married. I will not do any women wrong by mistrusting them, but I will do myself right by not trusting any women. The fine for the life I chose is that I must live as a lifelong bachelor, but since I need not spend money to support a wife, I may spend more money on my clothing and so dress finer.'"

"I shall see you, before I die, look pale with love," Don Pedro said.

"I may look pale, but it will be with anger, with sickness, or with hunger, my lord, not with love," Benedick said. "If I ever cease to be a red-blooded man and instead become a pale lover, then use a ballad-writer's pen to put out my eyes and make me blind and hang me up at the door of a brothel-house in place of the sign showing blind Cupid."

"Well, if you ever stop your belief in bachelorhood and get married, you will prove to be a notable subject of gossip," Don Pedro said.

"If that ever happens, then hang me in a wicker basket like a cat and shoot arrows at me," Benedick said. "Let whoever hits me be clapped on the shoulder, and called Adam after the famous archer Adam Bell."

"Remember this old saying: 'In time the savage bull will bear the yoke,'" Don Pedro said.

"The savage bull may bear the yoke of a farmer; but if ever the sensible Benedick bears the yoke of marriage, then pluck off the bull's horns and set them in my forehead," Benedick said. "The horns will show everyone that I have an unfaithful wife. And let a sign be hung around my neck, and in such large letters as they write 'Here is a good horse for hire,' let the words on my sign say 'Here you may see Benedick the married man.'"

"If that should ever happen," Claudio said, "you would become as mad as a charging bull — you would be horn-mad."

"If Cupid has not already shot all the arrows in his quiver at the licentious ladies in Venice, he will shoot one at you soon and make you quake with love for a woman," Don Pedro said.

"I look for an earthquake too, then," Benedick said. "An earthquake is just as likely."

"Your resolve not to be married will weaken and become more temperate as time goes on," Don Pedro said. "In the meantime, good Signior Benedick, go to Leonato, give him my compliments, and tell him I will not fail to show up for supper; for indeed he has gone to great lengths to prepare a feast."

"I have almost wit enough in me for such a courteous mission," Benedick said. He then started to use the conclusion of an old-fashioned, conventional, fancy, formal letter: "And so I commit you —"

"To the safe-keeping of God," Claudio continued the conclusion. "From my house, if I had one —"

Don Pedro finished the conclusion: "The sixth of July. Your loving friend, Benedick."

"Mock me not, mock me not," Benedick said, a little peeved that they had taken his joke and had teased him about his lack of courtesy toward women. "Quit fooling around. Your conversation is like a garment that is decorated with odds and ends of cloth, and your decorations are but lightly sewn on. Before you mock the conclusions of old letters — and mock me — examine your conscience. You will see that I am right, and so I leave you."

He exited.

Now that Claudio was alone with Don Pedro, he spoke seriously to him: "My liege, your highness now may do me good."

"My friendship for you is such that I am eager to learn how I may do you good," Don Pedro said. "Even if the lesson will take effort, I am eager to learn it as long as it will help you."

"Does Leonato have a son, my lord?" Claudio asked. Even though he loved Hero, he was practical and wanted to know if Leonato had a male heir who would inherit Leonato's property. If Leonato had no male heir, more property would come to Hero.

"He has no child but Hero; she's his only heir," Don Pedro said. "Do you love her, Claudio?"

"My lord, when we went onward to fight this war that has just ended in victory for you, I looked upon Hero with the eyes of a soldier. I liked her, but I had a rougher task at hand — I needed to fight rebels, not to turn *like* into *love*. But now I have returned from war, and now that war-thoughts have departed from my mind, I have room for love-thoughts of soft and delicate desires. These thoughts are all about how beautiful young Hero is and how I liked her before I went to war."

"You will act like a lover soon and bore your hearers by reciting love poems to them," Don Pedro said. "If you love fair Hero, enjoy your love-thoughts. I will speak first with her and then with her father, and I shall get her for you — you and she will be married. Isn't this what you had in mind when you began to speak to me after Benedick left us?"

"You know what I wanted, and you could tell just by looking at me that I am in love," Claudio said, "but I was worried that you might think that my love for Hero arose too suddenly. I was going to explain my love by telling you a long story."

"The bridge does not need to be much wider than the river," Don Pedro said. "You need say no more words than are necessary. In addition, the best gift is whatever is most needed. You want and need to marry Hero, and I will help make that happen. I know that we shall have some entertainment — a dance at which we will wear masks — tonight. I will disguise myself as you, and I will tell fair Hero that I am Claudio. I will tell her privately that I love her and want to marry her. She will agree — she will be taken prisoner because of the force and strong encounter of my amorous words. Then I will go to her father and get his permission for you to marry her. In short, and finally, she will be your wife. Let us put this plan into action immediately."

They exited in order to get dressed for the masked dance.

Leonato and Antonio, his older brother, talked together in a room in Leonato's house.

"Hi, brother," Leonato said. "Where is my nephew, your son? Did he make the arrangements for the musicians for tonight's dance?"

"He is working on it," Antonio said, "But, brother, I can tell you strange news that you do not dream of."

"Is it good news?"

"Time will tell, but the news appears to be good — very good. Don Pedro and Count Claudio, while walking in a path through thickly branched trees in my garden, were overheard by a servant of mine. Don Pedro revealed to Claudio that he loves my niece — Hero, your daughter — and meant to tell her tonight at the dance, and if he found her willing to marry him, he meant to seize the quickest opportunity to talk with you and get your permission to marry her."

Leonato was cautious; all too often conversations are misheard or misinterpreted. He asked, "Is the fellow who told you this intelligent and reliable?"

"He is a good sharp fellow," Antonio said. "I will send for him, and you can question him yourself."

"No, that will not be necessary," Leonato said, "but let us regard this as a daydream instead of reality until the marriage proposal has actually been made. Still, we should let Hero know about this so that she will be better prepared to answer if in fact she is asked to consent to marry. Go and tell her."

Antonio exited.

Antonio's son entered with musicians, and Leonato spoke to them:

"All of you know what you have to do.

"Pardon me, friend; come with me and help me.

"Good nephew, please work hard and with enthusiasm during this busy time."

In a room in Leonato's house, Don John, who was Don Pedro's illegitimate brother and who had been defeated in battle and then forgiven by him, was speaking with his loyal attendant Conrade.

"My lord, why are you so excessively sad?"

"The things that cause my sadness are excessive and therefore my sadness is excessive," Don John said. "I am illegitimate — a fact that limited how much I could inherit. I have recently been defeated. I have been forgiven — and not killed — by my victor, but he is keeping a close eye on me."

"You should listen to reason."

"And when I have heard it, what blessing will it bring to me?"

"If it will not bring you an immediate remedy for your sadness, then it can at least help you bear your suffering patiently."

"You and I were both born under the astrological planet Saturn, and so both you and I are moody and melancholy and saturnine," Don John said. "Therefore, I am surprised that you would attempt to cure my serious sadness with moralizing platitudes. I cannot hide what I am. I must be sad when I have cause and smile at no man's jests. I must eat when I am hungry and wait for no man's permission. I must sleep when I am drowsy and be a servant to no man. I must laugh when I am merry and flatter no man. In short, I must do what I want to do when I want to do it without regard for anybody else."

"True," Conrade said, "but you must not do all these things just yet. You need to restrain yourself until you can do these things without taking into account your brother, who now has power over you and is watching you. You have recently rebelled against your brother, and he has just now taken you newly into his grace and favor. To stay in his good graces, you need to behave yourself. Now is not the time for you to be your true self."

"I would prefer to be a noxious weed in a hedge than a cultivated rose in a flower garden," Don John said. "It better suits my mood to be heartily hated by all than to assume a fake behavior that will gain me unearned affection from anyone. I speak truly. Although I cannot be said to be a flattering, honest man, it must not be denied that I am a plain-dealing villain. I am trusted — as long as I wear a muzzle — and I am allowed my freedom — as long as I am hobbled with a heavy weight. My brother has forgiven me enough not to kill me, but he has placed restrictions on me. I have decided not to sing in my cage. If I had the freedom to use my mouth, I would bite. If I had my liberty, I would do whatever I liked. In the meantime, I want you to let me be what I truly am and seek not to change me."

"Can you make any use of your discontent?"

"I use it all the time because I am always discontented," Don John said, and then he looked up and added, "Who is coming toward us?"

Borachio, another of Don John's loyal attendants, came toward them.

Recognizing him, Don John said, "Do you have any news, Borachio?"

"I have come from a great supper yonder. Leonato is royally entertaining Don Pedro, your brother. I can give you news of an intended marriage."

"Is there anyway that I can use this information to create trouble?" Don John asked. "Only a fool would get married and so make his life unquiet. Who is this fool?"

"He is your brother's right hand."

Speaking with hatred, Don John said, "Who? The most exquisite Claudio?"

"Yes."

Again speaking with hatred, Don John said, "He is a handsome fellow! And to whom does he wish to be married? Which way does he look to find a wife?"

"His look has fallen on Hero, the daughter and heir of Leonato."

"She is a very precocious March-chick! This chick is very young. How did you come to learn this?"

"I was being employed as a perfumer," Borachio said. "To sweeten the air, I was burning sweet-smelling herbs in a musty room when Don Pedro and Claudio came in and talked seriously. I hid behind a wall hanging, and I heard that Don Pedro would woo Hero so that Hero and Claudio could wed."

"Let us go now," Don John said. "That may prove to be food for me and my discontent. That young upstart mightily helped defeat me in battle and so won much glory. If I can cross him in any way, I will bless myself in every way. Are you both loyal to me and will you both assist me?"

"To the death, my lord," Conrade said.

"Let us go to the great feast," Don John said. "Their happiness is all the greater because I have been defeated. I wish that the cook were of my mind and would poison all of them! Shall we go and find out what we need to do for me to get revenge on Claudio?"

"Lead the way, sir," Borachio said. "We will follow you."

# CHAPTER 2

## — 2.1 —

In the ballroom of Leonato's house, Leonato, Antonio, Hero, and Beatrice talked. Other people were also present.

"Was Don John at the feast?" Leonato asked.

"I did not see him there," Antonio replied.

"How sour that gentleman looks!" Beatrice said. "Each time I see him I am heartburned for an hour afterward."

Hero said, "Don John is of a very melancholy and ill-tempered disposition."

"An excellent man would be he who was made halfway between Don John and Benedick," Beatrice said. "Don John is too much like a portrait and says nothing, and Benedick is too much like the eldest son of a lady; he is spoiled rotten and always chattering due to his expectation of a rich inheritance. The eldest son always inherits the bulk of the estate."

"In that case," Leonato said, "half of Signior Benedick's speech would be in Don John's mouth, and half of Don John's melancholy would appear in Signior Benedick's face —"

"With a good leg for appearance's sake and with a good foot for dancing, uncle, or with two of each," Beatrice said, "and with enough money in his wallet, such a man would win any woman in the world, if he could get her good will."

She thought, *The French use "foutre" to refer to sex, and slang uses "money" to refer to semen. In addition, "will" is used in this culture to refer to "sexual passion." If a handsome man were capable of giving good* foutre *to a woman and had enough semen in his scrotum, such a man could win any woman in the world, if he could arouse her sexual passion.*

"Truly, niece," Leonato said, "you will never get yourself a husband because you are so shrewish with your tongue."

"Truly," Antonio said, "she is too curst — too ill-tempered."

"Too curst is more than merely curst," Beatrice said. "I shall lessen God's sending of gifts by being too curst. It is said, 'God sends a curst cow short horns,' but to a cow too curst he sends no horns. God punishes a curst woman by sending her a husband with a short penis."

"Therefore," Leonato said, "because you are too curst, God will send you no horn."

"No horn means no husband because a husband is capable of being horny and producing a horn," Beatrice said. "I am blessed and thank God every morning and evening on my knees because I have no husband. I could not endure a husband with a beard on his face. I had rather lie in bed between woolen blankets. Both beards and woolen blankets are scratchy."

"Perhaps you can find a husband who has no beard," Leonato said. He thought, *Benedick has a beard, and Beatrice is unlikely to ever marry him.*

"What should I do with a husband who has no beard?" Beatrice replied. "Dress him in my woman's clothing and make him my waiting-gentlewoman? He who has a beard is more than a youth, and he who has no beard is less than a man. He who is more than a youth is not for me, and he who is less than a man, I am not for him. Therefore, I will take pay from an animal trainer and lead his apes to Hell, as is supposed to be the punishment for a woman who dies unwed and without bearing the children whom she ought to lead to Heaven."

"Well, then," Leonato said, "will you go into Hell?"

"No, not into Hell, but to the gate of Hell," Beatrice said. "The devil will meet me there, like an old cuckold, with horns on his head, and say, 'Go to Heaven, Beatrice, go to Heaven. This is no place for you maidens.' So I will hand over my apes to the devil and go away to Saint Peter to be admitted into Heaven. Saint Peter will show me where the unmarried people sit, and there we will live as merrily as the day is long."

Antonio said to Hero, "Well, niece, I trust that you will listen to your father when it comes time to make the important decision about marriage."

Beatrice replied, "Yes, indeed; it is my cousin's duty to make a curtsy and say, 'Father, I will do whatever you wish.' But cousin, let your father choose for you a handsome fellow, or else make another curtsy and say, 'Father, I will do whatever I wish.'"

"Beatrice," Leonato said, "I hope to see you one day married to a husband."

"That will not happen until God makes men of some other material than earth," Beatrice said. "Wouldn't it grieve a woman to have to obey a piece of valiant dust? Or to make an account of her life to a clod of wayward, crumbly dirt? No, uncle, I want nothing to do with marriage. Adam and Eve's descendants populate the world; Adam's sons are my brethren, and I believe that it is a sin to commit incest."

Leonato said to Hero, "Daughter, remember what I told you. If Don Pedro asks you to marry him, you know what to say."

"The fault will be in the music, cousin, if you are not wooed in good time," Beatrice said. "He must woo you properly — at the appropriate time and in the proper rhythm. If Don Pedro is too importunate, tell him that measure, proportion, and rhythm are desired in everything, and so dance out the answer. For — listen to me, Hero — wooing, wedding, and repenting are like a Scotch jig, a slow and stately dance measure, and a cinquepace. The wooing of a woman is hot and hasty, like a Scotch jig, and quite fantastic. The wedding is like a slow and stately dance measure, full of state and tradition, and modest in manner and moderate in tempo. Then comes repentance, and the husband with his legs gone bad due to old age dances the cinquepace faster and faster as the time remaining to him passes faster and faster until he sinks apace — quickly — into his grave."

"Beatrice, you are very perceptive — your understanding is very sharp," Leonato said.

"I have a good eye, uncle," Beatrice said. "I can see a church by daylight — I can see what is obvious."

"The revelers are entering, Antonio," Leonato said. "Let's move aside and make room for them to dance."

Leonato, Antonio, Hero, and Beatrice all put on their masks as the masked revelers — Don Pedro, Claudio, Benedick, the singer Balthasar, Borachio, Margaret (a gentlewoman who served Hero and who loved Borachio), Ursula (another gentlewoman who served Hero), and others arrived. Each mask was elegant and did a good job of hiding the wearer's face.

Don Pedro asked Hero, "Lady, will you dance with me — a man who loves you?"

"Yes," Hero replied. "As long as you dance gently — without stepping on my toes — and look handsome and say nothing, I am yours for as long as we dance around the room and especially when I walk away in the steps of this formal dance."

"When you walk away after the dance, will you ask me to accompany you?" Don Pedro asked.

"I may very well do so, if it pleases me to do so."

"And when would it please you to ask me to accompany you?"

"When I know that I like your face," Hero said. "A lute is a beautiful instrument, but it is often hidden by the ugly case it is kept in. I would hate for your face to be as ugly as the mask that covers it."

"My mask is like the humble thatched cottage roof that kept the rain off humble Philemon, whose character was made of gold," Don Pedro said. "When the god Jupiter traveled the earth in disguise to test the hospitality of the people he met, Philemon and his wife, Baucis, gave the disguised god the best hospitality that they were capable of giving."

"If what you say is true, then your mask should be thatched with hair," Hero replied.

"Speak quietly, and let us speak about love," Don Pedro said.

They danced.

In another part of the ballroom, Balthasar said to Margaret, "Well, I wish that you would like me."

"For your sake, I do not wish that," Margaret said. She loved Borachio, but she also loved to tease other men. "I have many bad qualities."

"Name one."

"I say my prayers out loud."

"I love you all the more because of it. Those who hear your prayers can cry, 'Amen!'"

"I hope that God matches me with a good dancer!"

"Amen!"

"And I hope that God keeps him out of my sight when the dance is done. Answer me the way the congregation answers a good preacher. Say 'Amen!'"

"No more words. I have finished," Balthasar said.

They danced.

In another part of the ballroom, Ursula, who had recognized the masked Antonio, said to him, "I know who you are; you are Signior Antonio."

Antonio denied it: "No, I am not Antonio."

"I know that you are Antonio by the way you move your head. Due to your old age, it trembles."

"No," Antonio said, like many people at masked dances who deny that they are who they are. "I am imitating Antonio."

"You could never imitate him so well, including his old age, unless you were Antonio," Ursula said. "Antonio is an old man, and you are exactly like an old man from top to bottom. Your hands are his hands. You are Antonio, and Antonio is you."

"I am not Antonio," Antonio said.

"Come, come, do you think I do not know you by your excellent sense of humor? Can such an excellent quality hide itself? Stop denying it. Your good qualities have revealed that you are Antonio, and there is nothing more to be said about it."

In another part of the ballroom, Beatrice talked with Benedick, who had earlier recognized her by her voice.

Beatrice asked, "Won't you tell me who told you what you just said to me?"

Still disguising his voice, Benedick replied, "Please pardon me, but no."

"And you won't tell me who you are?"

"Not now," Benedick replied.

"Someone told you that I was disdainful, and that I stole my witty comments out of an old joke book titled *A Hundred Merry Tales*. Well, I know who told you that — it was Signior Benedick who said so."

"Who is Signior Benedick?" Signior Benedick asked Beatrice.

"I am sure you know him well enough."

"No, I don't — believe me."

"Hasn't he ever made you laugh?"

"Please, who is he?"

"He is Don Pedro's jester. He is a very dull and stupid fool. His only talent is inventing incredible slanders. No one but libertines who laugh at any joke delight in him, and they like him not because of his wit, but because of his villainies. He pleases some men by telling outrageous and villainous lies about other men, and then some men laugh at him and other men beat him. I am sure he is somewhere in this fleet of masked dancers. I wish that he had tried to board me with his wit — I know how to defend myself against his wit with my wit."

"When I become acquainted with the gentleman, I will tell him what you are saying," Benedick said.

"Do so," Beatrice said. "He will make a joke about me and scornfully compare me to something nasty. If no one hears him or laughs, then he will sink into melancholy, and not eat, thereby saving his host a partridge wing."

She listened to the music that started a new dance and said, "We must follow the leaders of the dance."

"In every good thing," Benedick said.

"If the leaders try to lead us to any bad thing, I will leave the dance floor at the first opportunity I get."

Benedick and Beatrice danced.

A little later, in another part of the ballroom, Don John and Borachio talked. Claudio was nearby, but out of hearing distance.

Don John said, "I have been watching my half-brother, Don Pedro. I know that he is wooing Hero for Claudio but anyone who did not already know that would think that he was wooing her for himself. I think I can cause some trouble now. Don Pedro has left the dance floor to talk to Hero's father and tell him that Claudio wishes to marry Hero. Actually, everyone except for we two and this one masked man has left the dance floor. The musicians are taking a break, and almost everyone is getting refreshments."

"I know who the masked man over there is," Borachio said. "He is Claudio. I can tell by his posture and the way he carries himself."

Don John and Borachio walked over to Claudio.

Eager to cause trouble, Don John asked, "Aren't you Signior Benedick?"

Often, people at masked dances lie to keep their identities hidden and have fun. Claudio did so now.

"You know who I am," Claudio said. "I am Signior Benedick."

"Signior Benedick, you are very close to my brother; he greatly respects you. Don Pedro is in love with Hero. Please, try to convince him not to marry her. Don Pedro is a Prince, and her birth is not equal to his birth. If you convince Don Pedro not to marry Hero, you will do a good deed."

"How do you know that Don Pedro loves Hero?" Claudio asked.

"I heard him swear his affection to her," Don John lied.

"I did, too," Borachio said. "Don Pedro swore tonight that he would marry Hero."

"Come, let us get some refreshments," Don John said.

He and Borachio left, but Claudio remained behind and said to himself, "I pretended to be Benedick when I spoke, but *my* ears are the ears that have heard this bad news. I believe what I heard. I am certain that Don Pedro, who greatly outranks me and to whom I have sworn my allegiance, loves Hero and has wooed her for himself so that he can marry her. Friendship is enduring in everything except when it comes to love. Therefore, all hearts in love ought to use their own tongues and do their own wooing. Let every eye negotiate for itself and trust no agent to negotiate a wedding. Beauty is a witch that charms the eye and turns friendship into rivalry. Such things as this happen every hour of every day, and I ought not to have trusted Don Pedro. Farewell, therefore, Hero! You shall be married to Don Pedro and not to me."

Benedick, who had heard the gossip about Don Pedro, now entered the ballroom and, seeing the masked Claudio, asked him, "Are you Count Claudio?"

"Yes, I am."

"Come, will you go with me?"

"Where?"

"We should seek a weeping willow — that symbol of unrequited love — because I have bad news for you. In what fashion will you wear your weeping-willow garland? Will you wear it about your neck, like a usurer's gold chain? Or over your right shoulder and under your left arm, like a lieutenant's scarf? You must wear it one way or another because Don Pedro has won your Hero. You may wish to continue to be his friend and grow rich from his bounty, or you may wish to challenge him to a duel."

"I wish him joy of her," Claudio said bitterly.

"You sound like an honorable seller of cattle — that is how they talk when selling a young castrated bull," Benedick said. Even now, he was unable to stop making unappreciated jokes. "But seriously, did you think that Don Pedro would treat you like this?"

"Please, leave me and let me be alone," Claudio said.

"Now you are acting like a blind man," Benedick said. "You are striking out and hitting everything close to you. A boy stole your meat, but in your blindness you are hitting a post."

"If you will not leave me, then I will leave you," Claudio said.

He exited.

"Alas, poor hurt fowl!" Benedick said. "Now he will creep into a bush and use it as a hiding place."

He paused and then added, "I am surprised that my Lady Beatrice should know me very well, and yet not know me when I was wearing a mask! She called me Don Pedro's fool! Really! It may be that I am called that because I am merry. Perhaps, but I think that I am doing wrong to believe her when she said that. I am not so reputed; no one but Beatrice would call me Don Pedro's fool. Beatrice has a base and bitter disposition that makes her believe that the entire world has the same opinion of me that she does. Well, I will be revenged on her as soon as I find an opportunity."

Don Pedro now entered the room and asked Benedick, "Where is Claudio? Have you seen him?"

"Indeed, my lord, I have played the role of Lady Gossip. I found him here as melancholy as a lonely gamekeeper's lonely lodge in a lonely warren. I told Claudio — and I think I told him the truth — that you had gotten the good will of this young lady and her agreement to marry, and so I offered to accompany Claudio on a visit to a willow-tree, either to make him a garland of weeping willow because he is forsaken by love, or to make him a rod because he deserves to be whipped."

"To be whipped! What is he guilty of?" Don Pedro said, puzzled. He had done what he had said he would do and had courted Hero for Claudio and had gotten her good will and her father's permission for Claudio to marry her. Now he wanted to share the good news with Claudio.

"He is guilty of the undeniable transgression of a schoolboy, who, being overjoyed with finding a bird's nest, shows it to his companion, who steals it," Benedick said.

"The schoolboy is guilty of nothing. Having trust in someone is a virtue, not a vice. The companion who stole the bird's nest is the guilty one."

"Nevertheless, it would have been appropriate for a rod to be made from a weeping willow, and for the garland to be made as well. Claudio could wear the garland himself, and use the rod to beat you because — as I understand it — you have stolen his bird's nest."

Understanding dawned on Don Pedro. Gossip is often wrong, and great men are often the subjects of gossip. He said, "My intention is only to teach the nestlings how to sing and then I will return them to their owner. Soon enough, people will be talking about Hero's marriage to Claudio."

"If what the nestlings say agrees with what you are saying, then I will know that you are telling the truth."

Don Pedro could have been insulted by this comment, but he knew and liked Benedick, who had recently fought bravely in battle for him, and one of the things that Don Pedro knew and liked about Benedick was his willingness to say plainly what he was thinking. Right now, Benedick was thinking that Don Pedro really wanted Hero for himself. No matter. Soon the truth would be known.

Right now, Don Pedro changed the subject: "The Lady Beatrice has a quarrel with you. The gentleman who danced with her told her that she is much wronged by you. The gentleman said that you insulted her."

"I am the masked gentleman who danced with her," Benedick replied. "She did not recognize me. I told her that someone said to me that she was disdainful and that she stole her witty comments out of an old joke book titled *A Hundred Merry Tales*.

"Of course, Beatrice being Beatrice, she immediately concluded that the insulting gentleman was me. Beatrice so abused me in words that even a block of wood would not endure it. An oak with only one green leaf on it would have revived and responded to her abuse. My mask seemed to come to life and answer her. She told me, not knowing that I was Benedick, that I was your jester. She told me that I was duller than a great thaw during which the roads are so muddy that no one can leave home and so is forced to remain at home and be bored. She kept firing jest upon jest with such incredible skill at me — whom she did not think to be me — that I felt that I was standing next to an archery target with a whole army shooting at it.

"Beatrice's words are daggers, and every word stabs. If her breath were as terrible as her insulting sentences, no one could live near her; she would infect the air from here to the North Star and the outer limits of the universe. I would not marry her even if she were endowed with all that Adam had before he sinned and was thrown out of the Garden of Eden. She would have forced Hercules to dress in women's clothing and turn the spit on which meat roasted and do other work in the kitchen — yes, and she would ahve broken his club and made firewood out of it, too.

"But let us not talk about her — she is a well-dressed but infernal Ate — the goddess of delusion and folly. I wish to God that some scholar would exorcise whatever demon possesses her. It is certain that while she is alive here on Earth, a man may live as quietly in Hell as he could in a sanctuary, and it is certain that people sin on purpose because they prefer to go to Hell for the peace and quiet rather than stay on Earth with Beatrice. Indeed, all disquiet, horror, and perturbation follow that woman."

Don Pedro said to Benedick, "Look, here comes Beatrice now."

Claudio, Beatrice, Hero, and Leonato walked over to Don Pedro and Benedick. Claudio was unhappy because he thought that Don Pedro and Hero were going to marry each other.

Benedick said to Don Pedro, "Will your grace command me to perform any service at the end of the world? I will go on any errand now to the opposite side of the Earth that you can think of to send me on. I will fetch you a toothpick from the furthest part of Asia. I will find the Christian emperor Prester John and measure the size of his feet and bring you the measurement. I will bring you a hair from the beard of Kubla Khan. I will embark on any embassy to the Pygmies. I will do any or all of these things rather than exchange three words with this Harpy named Beatrice. Do you have any such far-traveling task that you want me to perform?"

"No," Don Pedro said. "All I want is your friendship and company."

"Sir, here before me is a dish I do not love," Benedick said. "I cannot endure Lady Tongue."

Benedick exited.

"Beatrice," Don Pedro said, "you have lost the heart of Signior Benedick."

"Indeed, my lord, he once lent me his heart for a while," Beatrice said, "and I gave him interest for it. I gave him my heart, and so he received a double heart: my heart, which I gave him, and his own heart, which he lent to me and then took back. In fact, he won my heart and took it from me by using loaded dice, and so you may truthfully say I have lost it."

"You have put him down, lady. You have put him down with words."

"I hope that he will not put me down on my back, my lord, lest I should thereafter give birth to fools," Beatrice said, and then added, "I have brought Count Claudio, whom you sent me to seek."

Don Pedro looked at Claudio and noticed that he did not look happy. Don Pedro said to him, "How are you, Claudio? Why do you look sad?"

"I am not sad, my lord."

"Are you sick?" Don Pedro asked.

"I am neither sad nor sick, my lord."

Beatrice said, "Claudio is neither sad, nor sick, nor merry, nor well. Instead, he is as civil as an orange, and we all know that oranges from Seville, Spain, are bitter. If orange is the color of jealousy, then Claudio is jealous."

"Beatrice, I think your description of Claudio is correct, but if he is jealous, I swear that he has no reason to be jealous," Don Pedro said.

He then said to Claudio, "As I promised you, I wooed Hero in your name, and I have won her for you. I have spoken with her father and have obtained his good will. He approves of the match, so name the day that you will marry Hero, and may God give you joy!"

Leonato said, "Claudio, take my daughter and marry her, and with her take my fortune. Don Pedro has set up the match of you and my daughter, and may God bless this wedding."

Claudio was so surprised that he could not speak.

Beatrice said, "Speak, Count Claudio. It is your cue."

"Complete silence most perfectly announces complete joy," Claudio said. "I would be only a little happy, if I could say how much I am happy. Hero, as you are mine, I am yours: I give myself to you, and this exchange makes me ecstatic."

Beatrice said, "Speak, Hero, or, if you cannot, stop his talking with a kiss, and do not let him speak."

Claudio and Hero kissed.

Don Pedro said to Beatrice, "Lady, you have a merry heart."

"Yes, I do, my lord," Beatrice said. "I thank it, poor fool that it is, because it keeps me upwind of and safe from trouble. Look, Hero is whispering in Claudio's ear that he is in her heart."

"You are correct, and you are now my relative," Claudio said.

"Why, so I am," Beatrice said. "I am now your in-law. With marriage come new relatives and alliances. To the wedding altar goes everyone in the world but I — men must think that I am unattractive and sunburnt like a peasant woman who has to work outside all day. I may as well sit in a corner and sigh for a husband!"

"Lady Beatrice, I can get you a husband," Don Pedro said.

"I would like to have a husband who is of your father's begetting. Does your grace have any brothers like you? Your father must have sired excellent husbands, if a maiden could find them."

"Will you have me, lady?" Don Pedro asked.

Unsure whether this was a real proposal — her birth was not equal to Don Pedro's birth — and unsure how to act if in fact it were a real proposal, Beatrice took refuge in a joke: "No, my lord, unless I might have another husband for working days. You are too fancy to be my husband except on Sundays. But please pardon me: I was born to speak all mirth and no matter. From me, you get jokes, not serious conversation."

"Your silence most offends me, and your merriness best becomes you because, no doubt, you were born in a merry hour," Don Pedro said.

"On the day that I was born, my mother cried during labor," Beatrice replied, "but a star danced in the sky, and I was born with a horoscope that indicated merriness. May God give all of you joy!"

Leonato said, "Beatrice, will you do those errands I told you about earlier?"

"Yes, uncle," Beatrice said, understanding that he was a little embarrassed by the joking between Don Pedro and her and so wanted her to leave. She said politely to Don Pedro, "Please excuse me," and left.

Don Pedro said, "She is a pleasant-spirited lady."

"There is little of melancholy in her, my lord," Leonato said. "Beatrice is never sad except when she sleeps, and she is not always sad then, for I have heard my daughter say that Beatrice has often dreamed of unhappiness and then woken herself up with laughing."

"She cannot endure to hear tell of a husband," Don Pedro said.

"No, not at all," Leonato said. "She laughs at all who try to woo her and so they woo someone else."

"She would be an excellent wife for Benedick," Don Pedro said.

Surprised, Leonato replied, "My lord, if they were married, they would make each other insane within a week."

Don Pedro asked Claudio, "On what day do you want to go to church and be married?"

"Tomorrow, my lord. Time travels slowly — like an old man on crutches — until the love of Hero and me is properly recognized in a wedding ceremony."

"That is too soon," Leonato said. "Wait until Monday, my dear son, which is just a week away, and a time too brief, too, to properly plan a wedding."

Don Pedro said to Claudio, "You are shaking your head with disappointment at having to wait so long, but I promise you that this upcoming week will not be boring. I will during this week undertake a new labor of Hercules. He did such things as bring the three-headed guard dog Cerberus out of Hell, but I plan to make Signior Benedick and the Lady Beatrice fall in love with each other. When I am finished, they will feel a mountain of love for each other. I want them to be married, and I believe that I can accomplish it, if you three will only give me such assistance as I shall ask you for."

Leonato said, "My lord, I will do so even if it keeps me awake for ten nights in a row."

"So will, I, my lord," Claudio said.

"How about you, gentle Hero?" Don Pedro said.

"I will do anything that is respectable, my lord, to help Beatrice to get a good husband."

"Benedick is not the worst candidate for a husband that I know," Don Pedro said. "I can and do praise him. He is from a noble family, and he has proven that he is courageous in battle and has established that he has a good character. Hero, I will teach you how to influence your cousin so that she will fall in love with Benedick. In addition, I, with the help of Leonato and Claudio, will so work on Benedick that, despite his quick wit and his queasy stomach for marriage, he will fall in love with Beatrice. If we can do this, Cupid will be out of a job because we will take his glory and his job and become the gods of love. I will tell you my plan."

Meanwhile, Don John and Borachio talked and plotted together.

"The engagement has been made," Don John said. "Count Claudio shall marry Hero, the daughter of Leonato."

"The engagement has been made," Borachio said, "but I can stop the wedding."

"Anything that we can do to hurt Claudio will be like good medicine for me," Don John said. "I hate him, and whatever will make him unhappy will make me happy. How can you stop this marriage?"

"I cannot stop it by using honest means," Borachio said, "but I can stop it by using dishonest means. I can do this secretly so that no one will suspect me."

"Tell me how, briefly."

"I believe that I told you about a year ago that Margaret, one of Hero's waiting gentlewomen, loves me."

"Yes, I remember."

"I can, at any indecent hour of the night, have her look out of Hero's bedchamber window."

"What life is in that, that would be the death of this marriage?"

"You yourself can mix the metaphorical poison that will kill the wedding," Borachio said. "Go to Don Pedro, your brother, and tell him that he has wrongly and dishonorably behaved by arranging the marriage of the renowned Claudio — whom you will say that you greatly admire — to Hero, who you will say is a contaminated whore."

"He will not believe that Hero is a whore without some evidence," Don John said. "Can we manufacture any evidence that will seem to show that?"

"We can manufacture enough evidence to deceive Don Pedro, torment and vex Claudio, ruin the reputation of Hero, and metaphorically kill Leonato. What more can you want?"

"I will do anything to hurt those people."

"Here is what we can do," Borachio said. "Find a good time to talk in private to Don Pedro and Claudio. Tell them that you know that Hero loves me. Pretend to be very concerned about both men because you have learned this. Pretend to be worried about Don Pedro, who will lose honor because he arranged the wedding of Claudio to a 'whore,' and pretend to be worried about Claudio, who will lose his good reputation if he marries this woman who is, you will say, only pretending to be a virgin. They will not believe this without evidence. Take them outside Hero's bedroom window at a time we will set, and they will see me outside the bedroom window. They will also see 'Hero' — that is, Margaret — and me together. I will call her 'Hero,' since she and I sometimes pretend to be aristocrats — she sometimes calls me 'Claudio.' All of this will happen the night before the wedding. That will give me time to arrange a reason for Hero to sleep somewhere else that night. We will give them enough 'evidence' of Hero's disloyalty to Claudio that they will conclude that the 'evidence' is proof of Hero's disloyalty and whoredom. In that way, the wedding will be stopped."

"This plan will result in much evil, and I support it with all my heart," Don John said. "Be clever in carrying out this plot, and I will reward you with a thousand coins."

"As long as you play your part in the plot well, I will do likewise," Borachio said. "This plot will succeed."

"I will go immediately and find out on what day they intend to be married," Don John said.

Benedick stood alone in Leonato's garden. He called, "Boy!"

A young servant entered the garden and said, "Yes, sir?"

"On the sill of my bedroom window lies a book. Bring it here to me in this garden."

"I am here already, sir," the boy said, meaning that he would be back so quickly that it would be as if he had never left — a boast that he would not live up to.

"I know you are," Benedick said, "but I wish that you had left already, so that you could the more quickly return."

The young servant left to carry out the errand, and Benedick said to himself, "I do much wonder that one man, seeing how much another man is a fool when he falls in love, will, after he has laughed at such shallow follies in others, become what he has laughed at by himself falling in love. Such a man is Claudio. I have known when he would listen to no music but the drum and the fife of military music, but now he prefers the tabor and pipe music that is played at home. I have known when Claudio would have walked ten miles on foot to see a specimen of excellent armor. Now he will lie awake for ten nights planning which fashion a tailor should follow when making a new jacket for him. Claudio used to speak plainly and to the purpose, like an honest man. Now he has become a collector of pretty-sounding words. The words he uses are a fantastic banquet with many strange dishes. Is it possible that I will become so converted by falling in love and see things with eyes such as his? I cannot tell, but I think not. I will not swear to it, but love may possibly transform me into an oyster — the lowest form of animal life. But I will swear an oath that until love has made an oyster out of me, love will never make me such a fool as love has made Claudio."

He paused and then said, "One woman is beautiful, yet I am well. Another woman is wise, yet I am well. Another woman is virtuous, yet I am well. Until all these graces can be found in one woman, I will not fall in love with one woman. The woman I fall in love with shall be rich — that is certain. She must be wise, or I want nothing to do with her. She must be virtuous, or I will not make a bid for her. She must be mild, or I will not let her come near me.

She must be noble if I am to be an angel to her. She must be able to hold an intelligent conversation and to play music excellently, and her hair shall be of whatever color it pleased God to make it — it shall not be dyed or a wig."

He heard a noise, looked up, and said, "Ha! Don Pedro and Monsieur Love! I am not in the mood to hear about a wedding. I will hide in the arbor."

Don Pedro, Claudio, and Leonato entered the garden.

"So shall we hear Balthasar sing this song?" Don Pedro asked.

"Yes, my good lord," Claudio replied. "How still the evening is, as if it were quiet on purpose to honor harmony!"

Don Pedro whispered, "Did you see where Benedick has hidden himself?"

"Yes," Claudio whispered. "Once the song is over, we will give that hidden fox value for his money."

Balthasar arrived with a small band of musicians.

"Balthasar, sing that song again," Don Pedro said.

"My good lord, please do not tax so bad a voice to slander music any more than once."

"It is evidence of excellency to pretend not to know one's own perfection. Please, sing, and don't make me woo you any more."

"Because you talk of wooing, I will sing," Balthasar said. "Many wooers woo a woman he thinks is not worthy, and yet he woos her and swears that he loves her."

"Please, sing," Don Pedro said. "If you want to continue to make sounds, do so with musical notes."

"Note this before I sing my notes: Not a note of mine is worth the noting."

Peeved, Don Pedro said, "Why, these are very crotchety words that he speaks: note, notes, noting, and nothing else — I hear nothing of the song I requested."

Not wanting Prince Don Pedro to be upset, the musicians began to play.

Benedick, who was hiding, said to himself, "Now, divine music! Now is Don Pedro's soul ravished! Isn't it strange that lute strings made from the guts of sheep should draw souls out of the bodies of men and take them to a kind of paradise? Well, I prefer to listen to a hunting horn, when all is said and done."

Balthasar sang this song:

"*Sigh no more, ladies, sigh no more,*

"*Men were deceivers ever,*

"*One foot in sea and one on shore,*
"*To one thing constant never:*
"*Then sigh not so, but let them go,*
"*And be you blithe and bonny,*
"*Converting all your sounds of woe*
"*Into 'Hey nonny, nonny.'*
"*Sing no more ditties, sing no more,*
"*Of sad songs so dull and heavy;*
"*The fraud of men was ever so,*
"*Since summer first was leafy:*
"*Then sigh not so, but let them go,*
"*And be you blithe and bonny,*
"*Converting all your sounds of woe*
"*Into 'Hey nonny, nonny.'*"

Don Pedro said, "Indeed, that is a good song."

"And a bad singer, my lord," Balthasar said.

"Ha, no, no — you sing well enough for a makeshift."

Benedick disagreed with Don Pedro's opinion of the song and its singer. He said to himself, "If a dog had howled like Balthasar, people would have hanged it. I hope to God that Balthasar's bad voice is not a predictor of bad things to come. I would rather have heard the night-raven, predictor of ominous events, no matter whatever plague would follow its croaking."

The song had reminded Benedick of his relationship with Beatrice. He had not been faithful to her.

"Listen, Balthasar," Don Pedro said. "Please, get us some excellent music because tomorrow night we will have it played at the Lady Hero's bedroom window."

"I will get the best I can, my lord."

"Do so. Farewell."

Balthasar exited.

Don Pedro said, "Come here, Leonato. What was it you told me earlier — did you say that your niece Beatrice is in love with Signior Benedick?"

Claudio whispered, "Let us keep stalking our prey. Benedick is listening."

Claudio said loudly, "I never thought that Beatrice would love any man."

"Neither did I," Leonato said. "It is especially to be wondered at that she should so love Signior Benedick, whom she has always seemed to hate in public."

Benedick thought, *Is this possible? Is this the way the wind is blowing? Can Beatrice possibly love me?*

"Truly, my lord," Leonato said. "I don't know what to think about it, but I do know that she violently loves him. Her love for Benedick is past all understanding."

"Do you think that she is faking her love?" Don Pedro said.

"That seems plausible," Claudio said.

"Faking her love for Benedick?" Leonato said. "If so, never has anyone faked love as well as Beatrice."

"What signs of love does she show?" Don Pedro asked.

Claudio whispered, "Bait the hook well; this fish will bite."

"What signs, my lord?" Leonato said. "She cannot sleep and sits up at night — you heard my daughter tell you that."

"She did say that, indeed," Claudio said.

"How could she fall in love with Benedick?" Don Pedro said. "Your story of her falling in love amazes me. I would have thought that she would be invincible against all assaults of affection. I would have thought that she would never fall in love."

"I thought the same thing, my lord," Leonato said. "I especially thought that she would never fall in love with Benedick."

Benedick thought, *I would think that this is a trick, but the white-bearded Leonato is saying that Beatrice loves me. He is a revered old man; surely such an old man would not play a knavish trick.*

Claudio whispered, "Benedick has been infected by our lie. Let's keep up the trick."

"Has Beatrice told Benedick that she loves him?" Don Pedro asked.

"No," Leonato replied, "and she swears she never will. This torments her."

"You speak truly," Claudio said. "Hero told you that. Hero said that Beatrice said, 'Can I, who have so often treated Benedick with scorn, write to him that I love him?'"

Leonato said, "According to Hero, Beatrice says those words whenever she tries to write to Benedick. She is up twenty times a night, and she sits in her slip until she has covered a piece of paper with writing, my daughter says."

"Now that you have mentioned a sheet of paper, I remember something funny your daughter told us," Claudio said.

Leonato said, "You mean when Hero saw a piece of paper that Beatrice had written on and saw that she had written 'Benedick and Beatrice' over and over on it until she had covered the paper."

"Yes," Claudio said.

"Oh, Beatrice tears her letters into a thousand pieces," Leonato said, "and criticizes herself for being so immodest to write to someone who she knows would mock her. She says, 'I predict what he would do by knowing what I would do. If he were to write to me that he loves me, I would mock him even though I love him.'"

"Then she falls down upon her knees," Claudio said, "and weeps, sobs, beats her chest, tears her hair, prays, and curses. She says, 'Oh, sweet Benedick! I love you! God give me patience!'"

"She does that, indeed," Leonato said. "Hero said so. Beatrice is so overwrought with love that my daughter is sometimes afraid that Beatrice will do a desperate outrage to herself: This is the truth."

"It would be good if Benedick were to learn of Beatrice's love for him by some other means, if Beatrice will not herself tell him," Don Pedro said.

"Why?" Claudio said. "Benedick would only make a sport of it and torment the poor lady."

"If he would treat her that way, the world would be a better place if we hanged him," Don Pedro said. "Beatrice is an excellent and sweet lady, and everyone knows that she is virtuous."

Claudio said, "She is also intelligent."

"In everything except for loving Benedick," Don Pedro said.

"My lord, when intelligence and love combat in one body for supremacy, ten times out of eleven love will win. I am sorry for Beatrice. I am her uncle and her guardian, and I care for her."

"I wish that Beatrice loved me so passionately," Don Pedro said. "Despite the difference in our births and social ranks, I would make her my wife. Let us tell Benedick that Beatrice loves him, and let us hear what he will say."

"Is that a good idea?" Leonato asked.

"Hero thinks that Beatrice will die," Claudio said. "Beatrice said that she will die if Benedick does not love her. And she said that she would rather die than tell him that she loves him. And she said that she would rather die than stop her accustomed crossness toward him even if he woos her."

"Beatrice may well be right," Don Pedro said. "If she tells Benedick that she loves him, it is very probable that he will scorn and mock her love. As we all know, Benedick can be contemptuous."

"He is a very handsome man," Claudio said.

"He has indeed a fortunate appearance," Don Pedro said.

"Yes," Claudio said, "and I think that he is very intelligent."

"He does indeed show some sparks that are both witty and sensible," Don Pedro said.

"I know that he is courageous," Claudio said.

"He is as brave as Hector, leader of the Trojan army," Don Pedro said. "He shows wisdom in the managing of quarrels. He either avoids them with great discretion, or he undertakes them with a most Christian-like fear that makes him want to do the right thing."

"If he fears God," Leonato said, "he must necessarily keep the peace: If he breaks the peace and enters into a quarrel, he ought to do so only with Christian fear and trembling and a desire to act ethically."

"So he does," Don Pedro said. "In reality, Benedick fears his God. Fearing God is a good thing because it keeps us from doing sin. However, when Benedick makes some of his most notable and critical jests, he does not seem to fear God. Well, I am sorry for your niece. Shall we go seek Benedick, and tell him that Beatrice loves him?"

"Let us never tell him, my lord," Claudio said. "Let her get over her love with the help of good counsel."

"No, that is impossible," Leonato said. "Her heart will break first."

"We will hear more from Hero," Don Pedro said. "For now, let us not tell Benedick. I respect Benedick, and I wish that he would look at and evaluate himself — he would see how much he is unworthy to have the love of so good a lady."

"My lord, shall we go?" Leonato asked. "Dinner is ready."

Claudio whispered, "If Benedick does not fall in love with Beatrice after hearing this, I will never again trust my innermost beliefs."

Don Pedro whispered, "Let's trick Beatrice the same way we tricked Benedick. We will spread the same net for her and trap her. Hero and her gentlewomen attendants will have to do that. We will have good entertainment when Benedick and Beatrice each think that the other is in love, when that is not true — yet. I really want to see them meet. It will be a dumb show — a pantomime — because both will be too embarrassed to speak to each other. Also, their conversation together has consisted entirely of insulting one another, and they will no longer do that and so they will not speak to each other. Let us send Beatrice to call Benedick to dinner."

Don Pedro, Claudio, and Leonato exited, leaving the hidden Benedick alone.

Benedick came out from his hiding place and said to himself:

"This is no trick. They were talking seriously, and they learned from Hero that Beatrice loves me. They seem to pity the lady: It seems that her love for me is like a bow that has been fully bent — it is stretched to the limit. Beatrice loves me! I must return her love. I hear how I am censured and criticized. They say that I will be haughty if I learn that Beatrice loves me; they also say that she would rather die than show me any sign of affection. I never thought that I would marry. I must not seem haughty — happy are those people who hear about their faults and work to mend them. They say that Beatrice is beautiful; that is true — I can see that for myself. They say that Beatrice is virtuous; that is also true — I know of no evidence against it. They say that Beatrice is intelligent except for loving me. Her loving me may not be good evidence of her intelligence, but I swear that it will not be good evidence of any stupidity — I intend to be horribly in love with her.

"I may perhaps have some odd quirks and remnants of wit broken on me; people will tease me because I have railed for so long against marriage, but don't tastes change? A man may love certain foods in his youth that he cannot endure in his old age. Shall quips and sentences and written criticisms — paper bullets that come from the brain — keep a man from following his heart? No, the world must be populated with people. When I said that I would die a bachelor, I did not think that I would live to see the day during which I would marry.

"Look, here comes Beatrice! By God, she is a beautiful woman! I see some signs of lovesickness in her."

"Against my will, I have been sent to tell you to come in to dinner," Beatrice said.

"Beautiful Beatrice, I thank you for your pains."

"I took no more pains for those thanks than you take pains to thank me. If telling you to come in and eat had been too painful to me, I would not have come."

"You take pleasure then in delivering the message?"

"Yes, just as much pleasure as you can hold on the point of a knife — it is not even enough to choke a chattering crow."

Beatrice paused, expecting a witty though insulting reply. Not getting one, she said, "You have no stomach, either for food or invective, Signior Benedick? Then fare you well."

She exited.

"Ha!" Benedick said to himself. "She said, 'Against my will, I have been sent to tell you to come in to dinner.' What she said has a double meaning. 'I took no more pains for those thanks than you took pains to thank me.' That means the same thing as 'Any pains that I take for you are as easy as thanks.' If I do not take pity on her and love her in return, then I am a villain. If I do not love her, then I am not a Christian. I will commission a miniature portrait of Beatrice to be made and set in a lockct."

# CHAPTER 3

## — 3.1 —

After dinner, Hero and her two gentlewomen attendants, Margaret and Ursula, were walking in Leonato's garden.

Hero said, "Good Margaret, go to the parlor. There you will find my cousin Beatrice talking with Don Pedro and Claudio. Whisper in her ear and tell her that Ursula and I are walking in the garden and you overheard us gossiping about her. Beatrice will be curious about what we are saying about her. Tell her that she can eavesdrop on us if she sneaks into the latticework bower that is shaded by the intertwining, sun-ripened honeysuckle overhead. The honeysuckle grew because of the sun, but now like an ungrateful courtier it plots against its benefactor and keeps the sunshine from reaching the ground. Tell her that if she hides herself there, she can hear all that we say about her. That is what I want you to do. Do it well, and then leave the rest to us."

"I will make Beatrice come here and hide, I promise you, immediately," Margaret said before exiting.

Hero said, "Now, Ursula, when Beatrice does come, as we walk up and down here in this arbor, we will talk only about Benedick. Each time I mention him, praise him more than any man has merited. I will say to you that Benedick is madly in love with Beatrice. In this way, we can make one of Cupid's crafty arrows: It will be the kind that wounds — that is, makes someone fall in love — as a result of gossip that people hear."

Beatrice appeared and tried — unsuccessfully — to keep herself out of sight.

"Let's begin," Hero whispered. "I can see Beatrice now. She is like a bird that runs along the ground as she tries to get close enough to us to listen to what we say."

Ursula whispered, "The best part of fishing is seeing the fish with its golden oars — the fins — cut through the silver stream and greedily devour the treacherous bait. Now we are fishing for Beatrice, who I can now see has hidden herself in this arbor. Don't worry about me; I will do my part in our conversation."

Hero whispered, "Let's go near her. We want to be sure that Beatrice can hear the false sweet bait that we are casting toward her."

Hero said loudly, "No, truly, Ursula, Beatrice is too disdainful and scornful. I know that her personality is as defiant and wild as the hawks on the rocky cliffs."

"Are you sure that Benedick loves Beatrice so strongly?"

"So say Don Pedro and Claudio."

"Did they tell you to tell Beatrice that Benedick loves her?"

"They wanted me to tell her," Hero replied, "but I told them that if they wanted what was best for Benedick to advise him to wrestle with his love for Beatrice, and to never let her know about it."

"Why did you do that?" Ursula asked. "Doesn't Benedick deserve as good a bed as Beatrice lies on? Doesn't he deserve as good a wife as Beatrice would be?"

"By the god of love, I know that Benedick deserves as much as may be given to a man, but Nature has never made a woman's heart of prouder stuff than the heart of Beatrice. Disdain and scorn sparkle in her eyes, which undervalue what they look at, and she values her cutting wit much more than she values anything else — in comparison to her wit, everything else seems weak and unworthy to her. She is not capable of feeling love or affection for anyone else; she loves only herself."

"I think that you are right," Ursula said. "It is best that Beatrice does not know that Benedick loves her — if she did, she would make fun of him."

"That is true," Hero said. "I have never yet seen a man — no matter how wise, how noble, how young, how handsomely featured — whom she would not totally misconstrue and say that his virtues are faults. She would spell the man's name backwards the way that witches recite the Lord's Prayer backwards. If he had a light complexion, she would swear that the gentleman should be her sister. If he had a dark skin, she would swear that Nature, while attempting to draw him, let some ink drip and made a foul and ugly blot. If he were tall, she would swear that a lance had an ugly head. If he were short, she would swear that a miniature portrait made from an agate had been very badly cut. If he were talkative, she would swear that he is a weathervane blown by all winds. If he were quiet, she would swear that he is a block of wood or stone that is moved by no wind. Thus she turns every man the wrong side out, and she never acknowledges the truth and virtue that a man of integrity and merit has deserved."

"Such carping is not commendable," Ursula said.

"Indeed not," Hero said. "To be as odd and eccentric as Beatrice is cannot be commendable. But who dares to tell her that? If I were to speak to her and tell her that, she would mock me until I disintegrated into air and were reduced to nothing. Or she would laugh at me until my soul departed from my body. Or she would load me with her heavy wit until the weight crushed me. Therefore, let Benedick, like glowing coals that have been covered with ashes to preserve the fire during the night, consume himself with sighs and waste away inwardly. That would be a better death than to be mocked to death, which is as bad as to die by being tickled to death."

"Nevertheless, tell Beatrice that Benedick loves her, and hear what she will say," Ursula said.

"No," Hero replied. "Instead, I will go to Benedick and advise him to fight against his passion for Beatrice. Indeed, I will devise some honest slanders — some harmless lies — to stain Beatrice with. Perhaps some ill words will make Benedick stop loving Beatrice, although everyone knows that she is virtuous."

"Do not do Beatrice such a wrong as to make up lies about her, even if they seem to be harmless," Ursula said. "She cannot so entirely lack true judgment — not if she has so swift and excellent a wit as she is reputed to have — that she would refuse to marry so exceptional a gentleman as Signior Benedick."

"He is the best man in Italy with the exception of my own dear Claudio," Hero said.

"Please, do not be angry with me, madam, but I have to say that Signior Benedick is the best man in Italy when it comes to judging his attractiveness, bearing, intelligence, and courage."

"Indeed, he has an excellent reputation," Hero replied.

"His excellence earned his excellent reputation," Ursula said, and then she asked, "When will you be married, madam?"

"Tomorrow, and every day afterward," Hero replied. "Come, let us go inside. I will show you some of my clothing, and you can advise me what to wear at my wedding."

Ursula whispered, "We have trapped Beatrice the way that hunters trap birds. We have caught her, madam."

Hero whispered back, "If that is true, then love can happen by chance, as well as by other ways. Cupid makes some people lovers through the use of an arrow, and others through the use of a trap."

Hero and Ursula exited.

Beatrice came out from her hiding place and said to herself, "My ears are burning. Can this be true? Do people really criticize me so much for being proud and scornful? In that case, I say farewell to contempt and adieu to maidenly pride. People do not say good things behind the back of a person who is proud and scornful. But, Benedick, continue to love me because I will return your love. I will tame my wild heart and return your love. If you really do love me, my kindness shall convince you to bind our loves in the holy bond of marriage. Other people say that you deserve my love, and I believe it on better evidence than the gossip I have overheard."

In a room in Leonato's house, Don Pedro, Claudio, Benedick, and Leonato were talking. Benedick had shaved off his beard. (Earlier, Beatrice had said, "I could not endure a husband with a beard on his face."

Don Pedro, Claudio, and Leonato expected Benedick to be in love with Beatrice as a result of their trick, and they were looking forward to teasing him.

Don Pedro said to Claudio, "I will stay only until your marriage is official, and then I will go to Aragon."

"I will accompany you there, my lord, if you will allow me to," Claudio said.

"No, not so soon after your marriage," Don Pedro said. "You have pleasures to enjoy, and taking you away from your marriage so soon would be like showing a child his new coat and forbidding him to wear it. I will be bold enough to have Benedick accompany me because I enjoy his company. From the top of his head to the bottom of his foot, he is all mirth and laughter. Two or three times Cupid attempted to shoot him with an arrow and make him fall in love, but Benedick cut the string of Cupid's bow and so Cupid no longer dares to shoot at him. Benedick has a heart as sound as a bell and his tongue is the clapper — whatever his heart thinks, his tongue speaks."

"Gallants, I am not as I have been," Benedick said. "I have changed."

Leonato said, "I think that is true. You seem to be more serious now."

"I hope that Benedick is in love," Claudio said.

"That is not possible," Don Pedro said. "Not one drop of his blood is capable of being truly touched with love. If Benedick is more serious now, he must be broke and need money."

"I suffer from toothache," Benedick said, but he thought, *It is more accurate to say that I suffer from lovesickness. I am saying that I have a toothache to explain why I am different from the way I usually am.*

"Draw it out," Don Pedro advised. "Pull it out."

Hearing the word "draw," Benedick punned on "hanged, drawn, and quartered" by exclaiming, "Hang it!"

"You must hang it first, and draw it afterwards," Claudio joked. He thought, *Drawing is disemboweling, and quartering is being cut into four pieces — being hanged, drawn, and quartered is the punishment given to traitors. Benedick has been a traitor to love by refusing to fall in love.*

"Are you sad because of your toothache?" Don Pedro asked Benedick.

"The pain is caused by a little tooth decay," Leonato said.

"No one feels the pain except the person who has it," Benedick said. "People think that it is easy to solve someone else's problems."

Claudio said, "I think that Benedick is in love."

"I do not see any sign of love in Benedick," Don Pedro said, "except for his love of foreign fashions. He dresses like a Dutchman today, a Frenchman tomorrow, or in the dress of two countries at once. He can dress like a German from the waist downward and wear baggy pants while he dresses like a Spaniard from the hip upward and does not wear a jacket. Unless he has a love for this kind of fashion foolery, as he appears to have, he is no fool for love, as you say he is."

"If Benedick is not in love with some woman, then we ought to no longer trust the signs that traditionally show that a man is in love," Claudio said. "Benedick brushes his hat and cleans it each morning. What do you suppose that means?"

Don Pedro decided to tease Benedick, who he knew had recently shaved off his beard. He said, "Another sign of a man's being in love is that he pays special attention to his appearance. Has anyone seen Benedick visit a barber?"

"No, but the barber's assistant has visited Benedick," Claudio said. "You can see that his beard has disappeared — the old ornament of his cheeks has been used to stuff old-fashioned, homemade tennis balls."

Leonato said, "Indeed, Benedick looks younger than he did. The loss of his beard has been a fountain of youth for him."

"Not only that," Don Pedro said, "but Benedick has been rubbing his body with cologne. Is it possible to tell anything about him by smelling him?"

"Yes, indeed," Claudio said. "We can smell that sweet Benedick is in love."

"The best evidence that Benedick is in love is his seriousness," Don Pedro said. "Benedick used to always be a mirthful man."

"And when has Benedick been known to take such care in washing his face?" Claudio said. "Now he uses a cosmetic lotion."

"Yes, indeed," Don Pedro said. "When has Benedick been known to use any kind of cosmetics? I know what people say about him because he does that."

"Benedick's jesting spirit has turned into a string for a lute, a musical instrument used for playing love songs," Claudio said. "Strings are tuned with frets, and now Benedick frets. That is why he listens to melancholy music that is heavy on the soul."

"All of the evidence points to one conclusion," Don Pedro said. "Benedick is seriously in love."

"I know who loves him," Claudio said.

"I would like to know who she is," Don Pedro said. "I'm guessing she does not know him well."

"Yes, she does," Claudio said. "She knows his faults, and yet she is dying of love for him. She would love to die in his arms."

"If she dies in that position, she will be dying while lying flat on her back with her knees apart," Don Pedro said.

In this culture, "to die" was slang for "to have an orgasm."

"All of this talk is not curing my toothache," Benedick said. "Leonato, will you take a walk with me? I need to tell you eight or nine wise and serious words that these buffoons must not hear."

Benedick and Leonato exited.

"I swear on my life that Benedick is going to talk to Leonato about Beatrice," Don Pedro said.

"I think you are right," Claudio said. "Hero and Margaret have by this time played their trick on Beatrice, who has probably fallen in love with Benedick. When Benedick and Beatrice — two bears — meet, they will not bite one another as used to be their custom."

Don John walked up to the two men and said to Don Pedro, "My lord and brother, God save you!"

"Good day, brother," Don Pedro said.

"If you have time, I would like to speak with you."

"In private?"

"If it pleases you," Don John said, "yet Count Claudio may hear because what I want to speak about concerns him."

"What's the matter?" Don Pedro asked.

Don John said to Claudio, "Do you intend to get married tomorrow?"

Don Pedro said, "You know he does."

"He may change his mind after he hears what I have to say and knows what I know."

"If there is any reason why I should not be married, please tell me what it is," Claudio said.

"You may think that I don't like you," Don John said. "Judge whether I do after you have heard what I have to say — I think that your opinion of me will be better than it is now. I believe that my brother greatly respects you, and because of his respect for you he has helped you to become engaged to Hero — but his effort to help you has failed and he has wasted his time and labor."

"Why, what's the matter?" Don Pedro asked.

"I came here to tell you what is the matter," Don John said. "Briefly, and without unnecessary details, since the lady is not worthy of being long spoken about, Hero has been unfaithful to you."

"Hero?" Claudio said.

"Yes," Don John said. "Leonato's Hero, your Hero, every man's Hero."

"Unfaithful?" Claudio said.

"The word is too good to point out all the extent of her wickedness," Don John said. "I could say she has been worse than unfaithful. If you can think of a worse word, I can show you that the worse word also ought to be used to describe her. Restrain your disbelief and let me provide proof. Go with me tonight, and you shall see a man enter her bedroom window the night before her wedding day. If you still love her after seeing that, marry her tomorrow, but if you want to keep your honor, it would be better for you to remain single."

"Can this be true?" Claudio asked.

"No," Don Pedro said. "I don't believe it."

"If you dare not trust what you see with your own eyes, then do not say that you know anything. Go with me tonight, and I will show you both something that you can see with your own eyes. You will see enough to change your minds. When you have seen more and heard more, proceed accordingly."

"If I see tonight any reason why I should not marry Hero tomorrow in the church," Claudio said, "I will disgrace her in front of the congregation."

"And since I helped you become engaged to her," Don Pedro said, "I will join with you in disgracing her."

"I will disparage Hero no farther until you are witnesses that she is unfaithful," Don John said. "Bear this bad news calmly until midnight, and then believe what you see with your own eyes."

"The happiness of this time has been perversely altered," Don Pedro said.

"The happiness of this time has been unexpectedly ruined by evil," Claudio said.

"It is better to say that a plague of evil has been happily prevented," Don John said. "You will feel that way after you see what I have to show you tonight."

On a public street, Dogberry, who was the city's head constable, and Verges, an old man who was Dogberry's assistant, were talking to some newly recruited night watchmen whose job it was to maintain the peace of the city. Dogberry and Verges were paid to do their jobs, while the new recruits were unpaid: Acting occasionally as night watchmen was part of their duty as citizens. Also present was this book's author, who thought, *I am a magician, and I have turned myself invisible. I will take no part in the events of this book, except for one thing. Dogberry, Verges, and the other watchmen often make malapropisms — they humorously misuse words and often say the opposite of what they mean to say. I will use the magic of my right hand and of my left index finger (which mainly presses as needed the shift key) to sometimes make appear [in brackets] the right words after the wrong words that Dogberry, Verges, and the other watchmen use.*

Dogberry asked the newly recruited watchmen, "Are you good men and true?"

"Yes, they are good men and true," Verges replied for them. "If they were bad men and false, then it would be a pity unless they did suffer salvation [damnation] of both their body and soul."

"That would be a punishment too good for them," Dogberry said, "if they should have any allegiance [alleged defiance or disloyalty] in them, since they have been chosen to be night watchmen of the Prince's city."

"Well, give them their orders, neighbor Dogberry," Verges said. "Tell them their duties."

"First, who do you think is the man most desertless [deserving] to be a constable?" Dogberry asked.

"Hugh Oatcake, sir, or George Seacole, because they can write and read," the first watchman said.

"Come here, neighbor Seacole. God has blessed you with a good reputation: To be a handsome man is the gift of fortune; but to write and read comes by nature [nurture]."

The second watchman said, "Both which, master constable —"

"— you have," Dogberry finished, adding, "I know what you were going to say; I knew this would be your answer. Well, give God thanks for your good looks and don't boast about them. As for your writing and reading, use those when you have no need [have need] to use such vain [worthy and useful] accomplishments. You are thought here to be the most senseless [sensible (he meant to say "sensible," but "senseless" is accurate)] and fit man for the constable of the watch; therefore, you shall carry the lantern. This is your duty: You shall comprehend [apprehend] all vagrom [vagrant] men; you are to order any such man to halt, in the Prince's name."

"What do we do if a man will not halt?" the second watchman asked.

"Why, then, take no note of him," Dogberry said. "Ignore him and let him go, and immediately call the rest of the watch together and thank God you are rid of a knave."

"If he will not halt when he is ordered to halt, he is not one of the Prince's subjects," Verges said.

"True, and we watchmen are to meddle with no one except the Prince's subjects," Dogberry said. "You shall also make no noise in the streets; for the watchmen to babble and to talk while on duty is most tolerable [intolerable] and not to be endured."

"We will sleep instead of talk," a watchman said. "We know what watchmen do."

"Why, you speak like an experienced and very quiet watchman," Dogberry said. "I cannot see how sleeping would offend anyone; however, take care that your weapons are not stolen. As watchmen, your weapons will be bills, aka pikes. Well, another duty is that you are to call at all the ale-houses, and tell those who are drunk to go home and sleep."

"What do we do if they will not follow orders?"

"Why, then, let them alone until they are sober," Dogberry said. "If when they are sober they still do not follow orders, then you may say that they are not the drunk men you took them for."

"OK, sir," the watchman said.

"If you meet a thief, you may suspect by virtue of your office that he is no true man. The less you meddle with or interact with such men, the better it is for you because you will avoid becoming corrupted by contact with such evil men."

"If we know that a man is a thief, shall we not lay hands on him and arrest him?" a watchman asked.

"Truly, by your office, you may," Dogberry said, "but I think people who touch tar will be defiled; therefore, the most peaceable [peaceful] way for you to behave, if you do see a thief, is to let him show what he is and steal out of your presence."

"You have been always called a merciful man, partner," Verges said.

"Truly, I would not willingly hang a dog, much more [less] an even partially honest man."

Verges said to the watchmen, "If you hear a child cry in the night, you must call to the child's nurse and tell her to quiet the child."

"What do we do if the nurse is asleep and does not hear us?" a watchman asked.

"Why, then, depart quietly," Dogberry said, "and let the child wake the nurse with crying; for the ewe that will not hear her lamb when it baas will never answer a calf when he bleats [moos]. If the nurse does not hear her own child, she will certainly not hear you."

"That is very true," Verges said.

"You have one more duty," Dogberry said. "You, constable, are to present [represent] the Prince's own person. That makes you the boss. If you meet the Prince in the night, you may order him to stop."

"No," Verges said. "I don't think he is allowed to do that."

"I bet you five shillings to one that he can: Any man who has studied the statues [statutes / laws] knows that he can order the Prince to halt. That is, of course, as long as the Prince is willing to halt. Indeed, the watchmen ought to offend no man; and it is an offence to order a man to halt against his will."

"Yes," Verges said. "That is right."

"Ha! I am right!" Dogberry said. "Well, watchmen, good night. If anything important happens, call me. Keep your fellows' secrets as well as you keep your own. Good night!"

He added to Verges, "Let's go, neighbor."

A watchman said to the other watchmen, "Well, watchmen, we know our duty: Let us sit here on the church bench until two o'clock, and then go home to bed."

Dogberry remembered one more thing to tell the watchmen: "One word more, honest neighbors. Please keep watch around the house of Signior

Leonato. Because of the wedding being held there tomorrow, a great deal of bustle is going on there tonight. Adieu. Be vigitant [vigilant], please."

Dogberry and Verges exited.

Almost immediately, Borachio and Conrade appeared on the street. The watchmen, unnoticed by Borachio and Conrade, stayed in the shadows.

"Conrade!" Borachio said.

A watchman whispered, "Let's be quiet and listen to these people who are out so late at night."

"Conrade, I say!"

"Here I am, Borachio. I am standing by your elbow."

"My elbow was itching. I thought I had a scab there."

"Don't call me a scab. I will get you back for calling me that. What do you want?"

"Stand here with me under this overhanging part of a roof because rain is drizzling. I will, like a true drunkard — for there is truth in wine — tell you all of a tale."

A watchman whispered, "I suspect foul play. Let's listen carefully."

"Know that tonight I have earned from Don John a thousand coins," Borachio said.

"You must have done something evil to get it, but is it possible that any villainy should cost so much?" Conrade said.

"You should ask instead if it is possible that any villain should be so rich," Borachio said. "But when rich villains have need of poor villains, poor villains may ask for as much money as they wish."

"Still, I wonder how you could make so much money."

"You are showing that you are uninformed. You know, don't you, that the fashion of a doublet, or a hat, or a cloak, is nothing to a man."

Borachio thought, *By that I mean that a man is not identical to his clothing. Dress an evil man in a preacher's clothing and people will likely think that the evil man is a good man. Dress a woman in someone else's clothing and on a dark night other people may think that the imposter is the woman whom the imposter is impersonating.*

"It is just clothing."

"I mean, the fashion," Borachio said.

"Yes, the fashion is the fashion."

"I may as well say that the fool is the fool," Borachio said. "But don't you see what a deformed thief fashion is and how it robs young men of their money?"

A watchman whispered, "They are talking about a thief named De Formed. I have heard about him for the past seven years. He is fashionable and dresses like a gentleman. I remember his name well."

"Did you hear somebody?" Borachio asked.

"The noise was caused by the movement of the weathervane on this house," Conrade replied.

"As I was saying, do you see what a deforming thief fashion is? Fashion makes all the hot-blooded young men between age fourteen and thirty-five giddily change their clothes. Sometimes they wear the fashion of the Pharaoh's soldiers in a grimy painting. Sometimes they wear the fashion of the god Bel's priests in the old church-window — you remember that the King of Persia had these priests killed after Daniel denounced them because they worshipped a false god. Sometimes they wear the fashion of the shaven Hercules in the filthy, worm-eaten tapestry in which his codpiece seems as big as his club."

"I see," Conrade said. "I understand that a man can wear out clothing by wearing it and so make it unwearable, but that changing fashions render much more clothing unwearable. Fashion makes young men giddy, but hasn't fashion made you giddy, too? You have been distracted by talk about fashion and so have not told me what you wanted to tell me."

"That is not true," Borachio said. "The point that I wanted to make about fashion is that a person is not identical to the clothing the person wears. Tonight, I wooed Margaret, the Lady Hero's gentlewoman attendant. Margaret wore some of Hero's clothing, and I called her by the name 'Hero.' She leaned out of Hero's bedroom window as she bid me a thousand times good night. I am telling this tale badly — I should have told you first that Don Pedro, Claudio, and Don John witnessed me wooing Margaret — she and I had quite the friendly encounter! — from their positions in the garden. Don John arranged the whole thing."

"And they thought Margaret was Hero?" Conrade said.

"Two of them did," Borachio said. "Don Pedro and Claudio thought that, but Don John, who is a devil, knew that the woman I wooed is Margaret. Don John deliberately convinced Don Pedro and Claudio that Hero is unfaithful. He did that partly by the lies he told them. Those lies made them suspicious.

Don Pedro and Claudio were also deceived by the darkness of the night, which helped them to believe that Hero was being unfaithful. Most of all, however, they were deceived by my villainy. My actions confirmed the slander that Don John had cast against Hero. Enraged, Claudio departed. He swore that he would meet Hero, as he had promised, the next morning at the temple, and there, before the whole congregation, he would disgrace her by telling everyone what he had seen during the night. He swore that he would not marry her but would instead send her without a husband back to her father."

The first watchman had heard enough; he shouted, "We arrest you in the Prince's name!"

The second watchman said, "Someone, go and get Dogberry, the right master constable. We have here recovered [uncovered] the most dangerous piece of lechery that ever was known in the commonwealth."

Borachio thought, *This watchman probably meant to say "treachery" instead of "lechery," but considering the way I was wooing Margaret, "lechery" is quite accurate.*

"A thief named De Formed should be arrested, too," the first watchman said. "I will know him because he wears one lock of his hair long."

Conrade started to attempt to talk himself out of trouble: "Sirs, sirs —"

The second watchman said, "You will be forced to reveal the whereabouts of De Formed, I bet you."

Conrade said, "Sirs —"

"Do not speak," the second watchman said. "We order you to let us obey [order] you to go with us."

Both Borachio and Conrade knew that the watchmen who had arrested them were fools when it came to using language, but they also knew that they were legally arrested.

Borachio said to Conrade, "We are likely to prove to be a goodly commodity, being taken up by these men with their bills."

Borachio thought, *Conrade will appreciate the joke, although these watchmen will not. My sentence has two meanings, one legal and one commercial: 1) "We are likely to prove to be a valuable catch, now that we have been arrested by these watchmen with their weapons." 2) "We are likely to prove to be a valuable parcel of goods, now that we have been bought by these men with their bills of credit."*

Conrade appreciated the puns and replied with puns of his own: "We are a commodity in question, I warrant you."

Conrade thought, *Borachio will appreciate the joke, although these watchmen will not. My sentence has two meanings, one legal and one commercial: 1) "We are a catch that is subject to judicial examination now that we are under warranted and legal arrest." 2) "We are a purchase of doubtful value, I promise you."*

Conrade knew that the watchmen had the legal authority to arrest Borachio and him, so he did not fight them but instead said, "We will obey you."

The watchmen set off with Borachio and Conrade to find Dogberry.

# — 3.4 —

Hero was talking with her gentlewomen attendants, Margaret and Ursula, in her bedroom.

"Good Ursula, wake my cousin Beatrice, and ask her to get up," Hero said.

"I will, lady," Ursula replied.

"And ask her to come here," Hero said.

"I will," Ursula said as she exited.

"Truly, I think that your other rabato — your ornamented collar — is better than this one," Margaret said.

Margaret had worn this rabato the previous night when Borachio had wooed her.

"No, good Margaret," Hero said. "I will wear this one."

"Really, I don't think that this one is as good as the other one, and I think that Beatrice will agree with me," Margaret said.

"If she does, then she is a fool, and so are you," Hero said, not unkindly. "I will wear no rabato except this one."

"I exceedingly like your new decorative head-dress in the other room," Margaret said, "but I wish that the hair that is part of the head-dress were a trifle browner. In addition, your gown is unusually fashionable, truly, and I believe that although I have seen the Duchess of Milan's gown that is so well praised."

"Her gown is more fashionable than all the others," Hero said.

"Compared to your gown, hers is a fancy dressing gown," Margaret said. "Her gown has cloth of gold and cuts in the sleeves to reveal the even richer material underneath, and it is laced with silver and set with pearls. It has tight sleeves that go down to the wrist and loose sleeves that are draped from the shoulders. The shirts are trimmed at the hem with blue silk. Her gown is extremely fancy, but your fine, dainty, elegant, graceful, and excellent gown is worth ten of hers."

"May God give me joy when I wear it because my heart is exceedingly heavy!" Hero said.

"Tonight it will be heavier by the weight of a man as he lies on you," Margaret said.

"I am shocked!" Hero said. "Aren't you ashamed to speak like that?"

56

"Like what, lady?" Margaret asked. "I am not speaking of anything dishonorable. Marriage is honorable, and so is the wedding night. Marriage is so honorable that it is honorable even for a beggar. Your betrothed, Claudio, is honorable even before he is married. I think you would have preferred that I say that your heart will be heavier by the weight of your husband — not just any man — as he lies on you. And if all goes well, you will be heavier because you will become pregnant. But you know what I meant; you know I meant no offense. I was talking about the weight of your soon-to-be husband, and there is no harm in that — as long as it is the right husband and the right wife. Let the weight be heavy and not light because a wife ought to feel weight on her on her wedding night, and a light woman is a frivolous woman — a wanton, unchaste woman. Ask Beatrice what she thinks about this — here she comes."

Hero said, "Good morning, Beatrice."

"Good morning, sweet Hero."

"How are you feeling?" Hero said. "You sound as if you were out of tune."

"The only tune I am in is ill," Beatrice said. "I am sick."

"If you want a tune that is not ill, I recommend 'Light of Love,'" Margaret said. "That is a light, not heavy, tune, and it has no part for a man. It begins with clapping. If you will sing the song, I will dance it."

"'Light of love' means wanton," Beatrice said. "If you dance to that tune, you will have light heels — feet that are raised high in the air and wide apart. If your husband has lots of stables, he will also have lots of barns and because you and he will roll in the hay the result will be lots of bairns."

"That is an illegitimate argument," Margaret said. "I have no husband, and so I kick your argument away with my light heels."

"It is almost five o'clock, Hero," Beatrice said. "It is time you were ready. But truly, I am exceedingly ill!" She sighed, "Ho-hum."

"Are you sighing because you want a hawk, a horse, or a husband?" Margaret asked.

"If the word 'ache' began with and sounded like the letter that begins 'hawk,' 'horse,' and 'husband,' I would be sighing because I have an aitch," Beatrice said.

"Well, unless you have completely renounced your old views, there will be no more sailing by the North Star," Margaret said.

Beatrice was mystified: "What does the fool mean, I wonder."

Margaret thought, *I think that Beatrice is sighing because of a different reason than illness. I think that she is sighing because she is in love with and wants to marry Benedick. Unless she has renounced her view that she wants never to be married, then there is no more trusting in signs of love such as sighs — or in anything we used to believe in, such as that the Pole Star, aka the North Star, indicates where the North lies.*

"What means the fool?" Margaret said. "I mean nothing, but I hope that God sends all people their heart's desire!"

Hero knew that Margaret was talking — not explicitly — about Beatrice's being in love, so she decided to change the subject lest Beatrice grow suspicious: "These are the gloves that Claudio sent me; they have been excellently perfumed."

Beatrice said, "I am stuffed up, Hero. I cannot smell."

Margaret knew that Beatrice meant that her nose was stuffed up, but she made a joke out of "stuffed": "You are supposed to be a virgin, and yet you are stuffed. Has a man stuffed your womb with a baby? Something good can come from catching a cold!"

"God help me!" Beatrice said. "God help me! For how long have you made being a wit your profession?"

"Ever since you stopped using your wit," Margaret said, thinking, *You still don't know that we have tricked you into thinking that Benedick loves you.*

Margaret added, "Don't you think that my wit becomes me rarely?"

Beatrice knew that Margaret meant 'rarely' to mean 'splendidly,' but she decided to joke that 'rarely' meant 'seldomly': "Your wit is not seen enough; you should wear it in your cap so that everyone can see it. After all, fools wear coxcombs on their heads."

She added, "Truly, I am sick."

Margaret said, "Get some of this distilled Carduus Benedictus, and apply it over your heart: It is the only thing that will help you to get over a sudden nausea."

Carduus Benedictus was a medicine composed of Holy Thistle. Thistles have prickles, and Hero punned, "Margaret, you are pricking her with a thistle."

Margaret thought, *Wholly thistle is nothing but pricks, and I am thinking a lot about pricks today although not the ones on thistles. I have also been thinking about holes.*

Beatrice, of course, had been thinking about Benedick quite a lot recently, and she was suspicious because of the mention of Carduus Benedictus: "Benedictus! Why did you mention Benedictus? Does your mention of this Benedictus have some hidden meaning?"

"Some hidden meaning? No, there is no hidden meaning. All I meant is plain Holy Thistle," Margaret lied. "You may think perhaps that I think you are in love. No, I am not such a fool as to think what I wish, nor am I such a fool as to wish not to think what I can, nor indeed I cannot think, if I would think my heart out of thinking, that you are in love or that you will be in love or that you can be in love. Yet Benedick was just like you in his opinion of marriage, and yet he has become a man who is like other men: He swore he would never marry, and yet now, despite what he swore, he metaphorically eats his meat without complaining. I do not know how you are changing and being converted the way that he was converted to a new way of thinking, but I think that you are beginning to look with your eyes as other women do. You are becoming like other women."

Margaret thought, *Benedick swore that he would never marry, and yet he has fallen in love. The same is becoming true of Beatrice.*

"What pace is this that your tongue keeps?" Beatrice asked. "Your tongue moves rapidly. What are you trying to say?"

"The pace my tongue keeps is not a false gallop," Margaret said. "It is a real gallop and not a mere cantor. The pace of my tongue is true, and all I say is true."

Ursula entered the room and said, "Hero, get dressed. Don Pedro, Count Claudio, Signior Benedick, Don John, and all the gallants of the town have come to escort you to church."

"Help me dress, good Beatrice, good Margaret, and good Ursula," Hero said.

In another room in Leonato's house, Leonato was talking to Dogberry and Verges, who had come on official business. Leonato, who was the Governor of Messina, greatly outranked and was much wealthier than Dogberry and Verges.

"What do you want, honest neighbor?" Leonato asked Dogberry.

"Sir, I would have some confidence [confidential conference / confidential conversation] with you that decerns [concerns] you greatly."

"Keep it brief, please," Leonato said. "You can see that it is a busy time for me."

"Truly, it is, sir," Dogberry replied.

"Yes, in truth it is, sir," Verges said.

"What do we need to talk about, my good friends?" Leonato asked.

"Goodman Verges, sir, speaks a little off the subject," Dogberry said. "He tends to ramble because he is an old man, sir, and his wits are not so blunt [sharp] as, God help us, I would desire they were; but, truly, he is as honest as the skin between his brows. His eyebrows do not meet, and so we can see that he is trustworthy. Also, he has not been marked on his forehead as punishment for a horrible crime."

"That is true," Verges said. "I thank God that I am as honest as any man living who is an old man and no more honest than I am."

"Comparisons are odorous [odious]," Dogberry said to Verges. "*Palabras*, neighbor Verges."

Leonato thought, Pocas palabras *means "few words" in Spanish, and that is probably what Dogberry meant, but Dogberry said* palabras — words — *and he has been saying word after word without saying anything of significance.*

"Neighbors, you are tedious," Leonato said. He was eager to leave and go to the church for his daughter's wedding.

Dogberry did not know what "tedious" meant, but he was willing to guess its meaning: "It pleases your worship to say so, but we are the poor Duke's officers."

Leonato thought, *Dogberry meant to say that Verges and he are the Duke's poor — that is, impoverished — officers. These men are the Duke's officers — that is, they are Don Pedro's officers — and people really ought to feel sorry for the poor — unlucky — Duke because he has such sorry officers.*

Dogberry continued, "But truly, for my own part, if I were as tedious [wealthy and generous] as a King, I could find it in my heart to bestow it all on your worship."

"You would bestow all your tediousness on me?" Leonato asked.

"Yes, and I would do the same thing even if the tediousness were a thousand pounds more than it is; for I hear as good exclamation [acclamation] of your worship as of any man in the city; and although I am only a poor man, I am glad to hear it."

"And so am I," Verges said.

*They said that they are glad to hear it*, Leonato thought. *Grammatically speaking, they said that they are glad to hear that they are poor men. Both of them are poor men in more ways than one. Of course, Dogberry and Verges meant to say that they are happy to hear that I am acclaimed, and I am glad to hear that.*

"Please let me know what you have to say to me," Leonato said.

"Sir," Verges said, "our watchmen last night, excepting [respecting] your worship's presence, have arrested a couple of as arrant knaves as any in Messina."

Leonato thought, *Verges said that the watchmen have arrested a couple of as arrant knaves as any in Messina, excepting your worship's presence — that is, the watchmen have arrested a couple of knaves who are as arrant as anyone in Messina with the exception of me, Leonato. In other words, I am more arrant than the knaves these watchmen have arrested.*

Dogberry interrupted although Verges was telling Leonato what he wanted and needed to know: "Verges is a good old man, sir. He will be talking. As they say, when old age is in, wit is out. God help us! It is a world to see."

Leonato thought, *Dogberry is mixing up his proverbs. The proverb he is thinking of is this: When ale is in, wit is out. Unfortunately, his mangled proverb — when old age is in, wit is out — is often true.*

Dogberry complimented his friend, "Well said, neighbor Verges," then he said to Leonato, "Well, God is a good man; God must have a plan for Verges despite Verges' loss of his wits. If two men ride on a horse, one man must ride behind — no two men are equal in ability. Verges is an honest soul, sir. Truly, he is as honest as any man who ever broke bread; but just as we know that God is to be worshipped, we know that we must thank God for all things. All men are not alike — it is a pity!"

Leonato said, "Verges is not your equal." He thought, *That is true. As much of a fool as Verges is, he is not Dogberry's equal.*

"God gives us our gifts," Dogberry replied.

"I must leave you now and go to the church," Leonato said.

"One more word, sir," Dogberry said. "Our watchmen, sir, have indeed comprehended [apprehended] two auspicious [suspicious] persons, and we would like to have them this morning examined before your worship."

"Examine these men yourself, and then come and tell me later what you find out," Leonato said. "As you should be able to see, I am in a hurry."

"It shall be suffigance [sufficient]," Dogberry said.

"Drink some wine before you go," Leonato said. "Fare you well."

A messenger entered the room and said to Leonato, "My lord, they are waiting for you to give your daughter away to her husband."

"I will come immediately," Leonato said. "I am ready."

Leonato and the messenger departed.

"Verges, good partner, go and get the sexton Francis Seacole," Dogberry said. "Tell him to bring his pen and inkhorn to the jail. We will now examination [examine] these two auspicious [suspicious] men."

"We must do so wisely."

"We will not lack wit, I promise you," Dogberry said. He pointed to his head and said, "Here is something that shall drive some of them to a non-come."

If Leonato had been present, he would have thought, *Dogberry meant that he would make the two men non-plussed — so confused that they won't know what to think. Actually, I think that is the effect that Dogberry has on many people. Dogberry's word — "non-comp" — also brings to mind the Latin phrase* non compos mentis, *which means out of one's mind. A few minutes' conversation with Dogberry can have that effect on the hearer.*

Dogberry continued, "We need the learned writer to set down our excommunication [examination / conversation / communication] with the prisoners. Meet me at the jail."

# CHAPTER 4

## — 4.1 —

Don Pedro, Don John, Leonato, Friar Francis, Claudio, Benedick, Hero, Beatrice, and some attendants were in the church, ready for the wedding.

Leonato said, "Be brief, Friar Francis. Use only the short and simple form of the marriage ceremony, and afterwards you can say your homily and tell the new husband and wife their particular duties to each other."

Friar Francis asked Claudio, "Do you come here, my lord, to marry this lady?"

Claudio replied, "No."

Leonato said, "Claudio has come here to *be married to* Hero. You, friar, have come here to marry Hero to Claudio."

"Lady, do you come here to be married to this count?" Friar Francis asked.

Hero replied, "I do."

"If either of you know of any secret reason why you should not be lawfully joined together in marriage, I order you on your souls to say so."

"Do you know of any reason why we should not be married, Hero?" Claudio asked.

"I know of none," Hero replied.

"Do you know of any, Count Claudio?" Friar Francis asked.

"I dare to answer for him," Leonato said confidently. "He knows of none."

"Oh, what men dare do!" Claudio exclaimed. "What men may do! What men daily do, not knowing what they do!"

Benedick idly thought, *Claudio is making interjections. I remember learning from my study of William Lyly's Latin grammar that some injections are those of laughter — for example, ah, ha, he.*

"Stand aside, Friar Francis," Claudio said. "Pardon me."

He then said to Leonato, "Will you freely and without restrictions give me this maiden, your daughter?"

"As freely, son, as God gave her to me."

"And what have I to give you in return, whose worth is the equal of this rich and precious gift?"

Don Pedro answered for Leonato, "Nothing, unless you render her again."

Leonato thought that Don Pedro meant that the gift that Claudio could render would be a grandchild, but Claudio knew that Don Pedro meant for him to give Hero literally back to her father.

Claudio said, "Sweet Don Pedro, you teach me noble thankfulness and true gratitude."

He then said, "There, Leonato, take Hero back again. I will not marry her. Do not give this rotten orange to your friend. She is like an orange that looks good on the outside but is rotten inside. Hero has only the outward signs and appearance of honor."

Tears trickled from Claudio's eyes.

He said, "Look how she is blushing now like a virgin! With what false assurance and false display of truth can cunning sin disguise itself! Doesn't the blood that is rushing to Hero's face in a blush seem to be believable evidence of a virgin's simple virtue? Would you not swear, all you who see her, that she were a maiden, a virgin, after you witness this blush? But she is not a virgin. She knows the heat of a lecherous bed; she blushes because she knows that she is guilty, not because she is modest."

"What do you mean, my lord?" Leonato asked.

"I mean not to be married and not to knit my soul to a woman who has been proven to be a slut."

"Claudio," Leonato said, "if you, to test Hero, have overcome the resistance of her youth and have taken her virginity from her —"

Claudio interrupted, "I know what you are going to say. You will say that if I have slept with her that she embraced me as if I were already her husband, and that our formal engagement will help excuse the sin of premarital sex. No, Leonato, I never tempted her with improper suggestions. I always treated her the way a brother treats a sister; I always showed her only modest sincerity and appropriate love."

"Have I ever seemed other than modest or appropriate to you?" Hero asked.

"That is enough acting from you!" Claudio said. "I will denounce your false appearance. You seemed to me to resemble the virgin Diana, goddess of the Moon. You seemed to be as chaste as is the flower bud before its petals are fully opened. But you are more intemperate in your sexual passion than Venus, goddess of love, or those pampered horses that are known to rage in savage sensuality."

"Are you ill?" Hero said. "Is that what is making you say things that are so far from being the truth?"

Leonato said to Don Pedro, "Sweet Prince, why aren't you saying something?"

"What should I say?" Don Pedro replied. "I am dishonored because I have helped my dear friend to become engaged to a common prostitute."

"Do I really hear these words, or am I dreaming?" Leonato asked.

Don John replied, "Sir, these words have really been spoken, and these things are true."

Benedick thought, *This does not look like a wedding.*

"You say that these things are true!" Hero said. "Oh, God!"

"Leonato, do you see me standing here?" Claudio asked. "Do you see Don Pedro standing here? Is this Don Pedro's brother standing here? Is this face Hero's face? Are our eyes our own? The answer to all these questions is yes. You are awake; you are not dreaming."

"I agree that I am awake, but what is going on here, Count Claudio?"

"Let me but ask your daughter one question, and, by that fatherly and kindly power that you have over her, tell her to answer truly," Claudio said.

"I order you to answer his question truthfully, Hero, my daughter," Leonato said.

"May God defend me!" Hero said. "I am attacked from all sides! What kind of catechising do you call this?"

"The first question of the Church of England Catechism is this: 'What is your name?'" Claudio said. "I will ask you one question that will reveal what your real name is."

He thought, *Your real name is a common one: Whore.*

Hero replied, "Isn't my name Hero? Who can blot that name with any just reproach?"

"I know the answer to that question," Claudio said. "Hero can blot her own name. Hero can blot out the virtue of Hero. Here is my question: What man did you talk with last night between the hours of midnight and one a.m. at your bedroom window? If you are a virgin, answer this question."

"I talked with no man at that hour," Hero replied.

"Why, then you are no virgin," Don Pedro said. "Leonato, I am sorry you must hear this bad news: Upon my honor, I, Don John, and this grieving Count Claudio saw Hero and heard Hero at that hour last night talk with a ruffian at her bedroom window. That man, a lecherous villain, stated that he and Hero had enjoyed a thousand vile encounters in secret."

"Those thousand vile encounters are not to be spoken of," Don John said. "The language that must be used to speak about those encounters would offend everyone who heard it. Pretty lady, I am sorry that you have been so lewd and unchaste."

"Hero, if you were only half as beautiful inside as you are outside, you would have been like the mythical Hero, who committed suicide after her loved one, Leander, died while attempting to swim the Hellespont to visit her," Claudio said. "But farewell, most foul and most fair Hero. Farewell, you woman of pure impiety and impious purity! Because of you, I will stay away from love. My eyes shall be suspicious. Every time I look at a beautiful woman I will think of impurity. Never again will I be gracious to a beautiful woman."

"Does any man here have a dagger that will stab me?" Leonato asked.

Hero fainted.

"How are you, Hero?" Beatrice asked. "Why have you fainted?"

Don John said, "Come, let us go. These evil things that have been revealed to the light of day have overwhelmed her."

Don Pedro, Don John, and Claudio exited.

Benedick normally would have left with Don Pedro and Claudio, but he loved Beatrice, and Beatrice was here, so he stayed.

Benedick asked Beatrice, "How is Hero?"

"Dead, I think," Beatrice replied. "Help, uncle! Hero! Wake up, Hero! Uncle! Signior Benedick! Friar!"

"Fate, let her die!" Leonato said. "Death is the fairest cover for her shame that I can now ask for."

"Hero, wake up!" Beatrice said.

"Take comfort in being alive, lady," Friar Francis said to Hero as she slowly regained consciousness.

Leonato said to Hero as she lay on the floor of the church, "Are you looking up?"

"Yes," Friar Francis said. "That is good."

"Good?" Leonato said. "It is hardly good. Why, doesn't every earthly thing cry shame upon her? Can she deny the guilt that her blushes reveal? Do not live, Hero. Do not open your eyes. If I did not think that you would not quickly die, if I thought that your spirit could bear your shame, I myself would kill you. If the army of your shames is not enough to kill you, I would act as the rearguard of the army and kill you.

"I used to grieve because I had only one child. I used to be angry at Nature because I had only one child. But when that child is Hero, one child is too many! Why did I have a child? Why did I ever think you were lovely? It would have been better if instead of having you, I had been charitable and adopted the child of a beggar who came to my gates. That way, when the child sinned and ruined her reputation, I might have said, 'No part of this child is mine; this shameful child has come from unknown loins.' But you were my own child and I loved you and I praised you and I was proud of you. For you I had such great love that I had little love for myself. But now Hero has fallen into a pit of ink and the wide sea has too little water to wash her clean again and not enough salt to preserve her and keep her from stinking."

"Sir, sir, be patient," Benedick said. "Calm down. As for me, I am so amazed that I do not know what to say."

"I swear on my soul that Hero has been slandered," Beatrice said.

Benedick said to Beatrice, "In our culture, it is normal for two unmarried adults of the same sex to sleep in the same bed. Did you and Hero sleep in the same bed last night?"

"No, we did not," Beatrice replied, "but for the entire year before last night we slept in the same bed."

"This confirms Count Claudio's story!" Leonato said. "Before, the story was so strong that it was as if it were made with ribs of iron! But now it is even stronger! Would the two Princes — Don Pedro and Don John — lie, and Claudio lie, a man who so loved Hero that he cried while speaking of her foulness? Let us leave Hero! Let her die!"

Friar Francis said, "Listen to me for a minute. I have kept quiet too long about these events. I have been looking at Hero, and I have seen a thousand blushes begin to appear in her cheeks only to be swept away by innocent and angelic paleness. And in her eyes has appeared a fire that burns against the lies that these Princes told against the truth of her virginity.

"Call me a fool and do not trust either my education or my observations, which combined with my years of experience have given me knowledge. Do not trust my age, reputation, position, or holiness. You can do all of these things to me if I am wrong and Hero turns out to be guilty.

"I believe completely that Hero is innocent."

Leonato said, "Friar, she cannot be innocent. The only good quality that she has left is that she will not add the sin of perjury to her damnation. Hero has not denied that she is unchaste. Why are you trying to cover up her guilt when she has been proven to be guilty?"

Friar Francis said to Hero, who had fully regained consciousness, "With which man are you accused of sinning?"

"I don't know," Hero replied. "You will have to ask those who accuse me. If I know more of any man alive than that which a virgin's modesty allows, let all my sins be unforgiven and let me be damned!"

She said to Leonato, "Father, if you can prove that any man has ever talked with me at an indecent hour or that I talked to any man last night, then disown me, hate me, and torture me to death!"

"Don Pedro and Don John have made some kind of mistake," Friar Francis said. "They have made a strange misunderstanding."

Benedick said, "Two of the three men who have accused Hero of unchasteness are completely honorable. If they have been misled, they have been misled by Don John the bastard, who enjoys creating conflicts."

"I don't know what to believe," Leonato said. "If these three men have spoken the truth about my daughter, I will tear her to pieces with my own hands, but if they have wronged her with slander, even the highest ranking of them will hear from me. Time has not yet dried up my blood, age has not yet eaten my intelligence, fortune has not been my enemy, and my faults have not bereft me of all my friends. These three men will find that I, awakened in such a matter, have enough strength of limb and policy of mind, as well as ability in means and choice of friends, that I will be able to thoroughly get revenge on them."

"Wait a while before you act to get revenge," Friar Francis said. "Listen to my advice now. Don Pedro, Don John, and Claudio left your daughter when she seemed to be dead. Let her for a while be secretly kept indoors in your house, and tell everyone that she is dead. Ostentatiously mourn her, and on your family's old tomb hang mournful epitaphs and do all the rites that are proper for a burial."

"Why?" Leonato asked. "What is the purpose of doing this?"

"If this plan works well," Friar Francis said, "slander will change to remorse. That will be good, but it is not the main thing that we will be hoping for. We hope for a better result. Because Hero died — we will say — at the same moment in which she was accused, she shall be lamented, pitied, and excused by every hearer. It commonly happens that what we have we do not properly prize while we have and enjoy it. But once it is lost and we lack it, then we greatly value it and recognize the good qualities that it has that we did not previously recognize. This will happen to Claudio. When he hears that Hero died because of his words of accusation, he will remember her and think about her. He will remember all of Hero's good qualities and even exaggerate them. It will be as if they appear before him in new and rich clothing. She will appear in his mind more moving, more delicate, and fuller of life than she was when she was alive. Then Claudio will mourn, if love for Hero was ever in his heart, and he will wish that he had not accused her of being unchaste, not even if he thinks that the accusation is true. Let us follow this plan. Chances are, things will turn out even better than I hope. If nothing else, people will talk about Hero's death rather than her supposed unchasteness. And if things do not work out, then you, Claudio, can keep her hidden, as would be best because of her ruined reputation, in some reclusive and religious convent, away from all eyes, gossip, thoughts, and insults."

Benedick said, "Signior Leonato, take the friar's advice. Though you know how much I respect Don Pedro and Claudio, I swear that I will participate in this plan as secretly and justly as your own soul and body."

"I am drowning in grief, and I will grasp at even the thinnest string I can find and hope to be drawn to safety," Leonato said.

"It is good that you agree to participate in this plan," Friar Francis said to Leonato. "Let us leave immediately. Strange illnesses require strange cures. Come, Hero, you must die in order to live. Your wedding perhaps is only postponed. Have patience, be calm, and endure these present ills."

Everyone except for Benedick and Beatrice left.

Benedick said gently, "Lady Beatrice, have you been crying all this time?"

"Yes, and I will cry a while longer."

"I do not want you to cry."

"What you want does not matter," Beatrice replied. "I am crying because I want to cry."

"I truly believe that Hero has been wronged."

"A man who could make things right would deserve much from me," Beatrice said.

"Is there any way I can deserve such a reward?"

"The way to earn such a reward is very straightforward and direct, but it is not for you," Beatrice said.

"May a man do it?"

"It is the duty of a man, but it is not your duty."

"I love nothing in the world as much I love you," Benedick said. "Isn't that strange?"

"It is as strange as another thing that I don't understand: It is as possible for me to say that I love nothing as much as I love you — but do not believe what I just said. I confess nothing, and I deny nothing. I feel sorry for my cousin."

"I swear by my sword, Beatrice, that you love me."

"Do not swear. You may have to eat your words."

"I swear by my sword, Beatrice, that you love me, and I will make anyone who says that I do not love you eat my sword."

"Won't you go back on your vow that you love me and eat your words?"

"I will not eat my words with any sauce that can be prepared to season them," Benedick said. "I swear again that I love you."

"Why, then God forgive me!"

"For what offence, Beatrice?"

"Your swearing that you love me came in a happy hour. I was about to go against our societal conventions and say to you 'I love you' before you — the man — confessed to me that you love me."

"Say to me now what you were going to say to me before, and swear to it with all of your heart," Benedick said.

"I love you with so much of my heart that none of my heart is left to swear with."

"Tell me to do anything for you."

"Kill Claudio," Beatrice replied.

"Not for all the whole wide world."

"You kill me by saying no," Beatrice said. "Farewell."

"Stay for a while, sweet Beatrice."

"I am gone, though I am physically here. There is no love in you for me. Therefore, please let me go."

"Beatrice —"

"I am leaving."

"Let us part as friends."

"You must think that it is easier to be friends with me than to fight Claudio, who is now my enemy."

"Is Claudio your enemy?"

"Why shouldn't he be?" Beatrice asked. "Hasn't he proved himself to be a thorough villain, one who has slandered, scorned, and dishonored my cousin Hero? I wish that I were a man! Look at what Claudio has done! He held Hero's hands until they were in church to join hands in marriage, and then with barefaced slander and unmitigated rancor he publicly accused her of unchasteness. I wish I were a man! If I were, I would eat Claudio's heart in the public marketplace."

"Listen to me, Beatrice —"

"Talk with a man outside her bedroom window! A likely story!"

"But Beatrice —"

"Sweet Hero! She has been wronged, she has been slandered, she has been undone."

"Bea —"

"The three men who accused her are two Princes and a Count! Surely, we heard a Princely testimony and testimony from a goodly Count — Count Candy! He is a sweet gallant, surely! Oh, I wish that I were a man for his sake! Or that I had any friend who would be a man for my sake! But manhood has melted into curtsies, valor has melted into compliment, and men are composed only of talk and not deeds — and such pretty talk, too. A man is now considered to be as valiant as Hercules even if he only tells a lie and swears that it is true. I cannot become a man by wishing I were a man; therefore, I will die a woman by grieving."

"Wait, good Beatrice. I swear by this hand that I love you."

"If you want to show that you love me, you will have to do more with your hand than swear by it."

"Do you truly believe in your soul that Count Claudio has wronged Hero?"

"I am as sure of that as I am sure that I have a thought or a soul."

"That is enough," Benedick said. "I will do what you want me to do: I will challenge Claudio to a duel. Let me kiss your hand, and so I leave you. I swear by this hand that he shall pay dearly for his sin. As you hear of me, so think of me. Judge me by my actions, not by my words. Go and comfort Hero. I must tell other people that she is dead, and so, farewell."

He kissed her hand and exited. Beatrice left to go and comfort Hero.

In a prison, Dogberry, Verges, and the sexton were wearing their official black gowns. Some watchmen were also present, as were Conrade and Borachio.

Dogberry asked, "Is our whole dissembly [assembly] present?"

"We need a stool and a cushion for the sexton," Verges said.

A stool and a cushion were brought for the sexton.

The sexton asked, "Who are the malefactors?"

"That would be my partner and me," Dogberry said.

"That is true," Verges said. "We have been exhibitioned [commissioned] to examine these men."

The sexton smiled, realizing that neither Dogberry nor Verges understood the meaning of the word "malefactors."

The sexton said, "But who are the offenders who are to be examined? Let them come before Dogberry, the master constable."

"Yes, let them come before me," Dogberry said.

Conrade and Borachio stood up, and Dogberry asked Borachio, "What is your name, friend?"

"Borachio."

Dogberry said to the sexton, "Please, write down 'Borachio.'" Then he asked Conrade, "And what is your name?"

"I am a gentleman, sir, and my name is Conrade."

"Write down 'master gentleman Conrade.' Men, do you serve God and obey His laws?"

Conrade and Borachio replied, "Yes, sir, we hope we do."

Dogberry said to the sexton, "Write down that they hope they serve God, and write God first; for God defend [forbid] that such villains should be named before God."

He then said to Conrade and Borachio, "Masters, it has been proven already that you are little better than lying criminals; and soon people will think that you are lying criminals. How do you defend yourselves?"

Conrade replied, "Sir, we say that we are not lying criminals."

Dogberry said to Verges and the sexton, "He is a marvelously intelligent fellow, I assure you, but I will outwit him."

He said to Borachio, "Come here and let me speak to you away from Conrade. I say to you, it is thought that you are lying criminals."

"Sir, I say to you that we are not lying criminals."

"Well, stand aside," Dogberry said. "By God, they are both telling the same story!"

He said to the sexton, "Have you written down that they are not lying criminals?"

The sexton replied, "Master constable Dogberry, you are not carrying out the investigation in the right way. You need to talk to the watchmen who are accusing these two men."

"Yes, that is the eftest [deftest / quickest] way," Dogberry said. "Let the watchmen come forth. Masters, I order you, in the name of the Prince, to accuse these men."

The first watchmen said, "This man — Borachio — said, sir, that Don John, Don Pedro's brother, is a villain."

"Write down that Don John is a villain," Dogberry said.

He thought a moment, reflected that Don John had a high rank, and then he said, "Why, this is obvious perjury [slander], to call a Prince's brother a villain."

If Don John had been present, he would have thought, *No, it is not slander. I really am a villain.*

Borachio said, "Master constable —"

"Please be quiet," Dogberry said. "I do not like the way you look, I promise you."

The sexton, who had decided that he ought to take over the investigation, asked the second watchman, "Did you hear this accused man say anything else?"

"He said that he had received a thousand coins from Don John in return for falsely accusing the Lady Hero."

"Being paid for falsely accusing the Lady Hero is as obvious burglary [fraud / being paid to slander someone] as was ever committed," Dogberry said.

"Yes, it is," Verges agreed.

"What else did you two learn?" the sexton asked the two watchmen.

"We learned that Count Claudio, who believed the slander, intended to disgrace Hero before the whole congregation in the church and not marry her," the first watchman said.

Dogberry said to Borachio, "Villain! You will be condemned to everlasting redemption [damnation] for this."

"Did you two learn anything else?"

"That is everything we learned," a watchman said.

The sexton said to Conrade and Borachio, "And here is more, masters, than you can deny. This morning Don John secretly fled from the city. Apparently, he was aware that you two had been arrested and that his evil plot would be revealed. Hero was accused in the manner you described, and as you described, Count Claudio refused to marry her. Because of the grief she suffered, Hero died."

The sexton said to Dogberry, "Master constable, let these men be bound and be brought quickly to Leonato's house. I will go there now ahead of you and tell him the result of our investigation."

The sexton exited.

Dogberry said, "Let the prisoners be opinioned [pinioned / bound]."

"Let's bind their hands," Verges said.

Dogberry moved toward Conrade, who had not taken part in Don John's evil plot and so was innocent. Conrade objected to being bound and shouted, "Back off, coxcomb! Get away from me, fool!"

Dogberry asked, "Where's the sexton? He should write down that the law-enforcement officer is a coxcomb. Well, let us bind their hands."

He said to Conrade, "You are resisting arrest."

Conrade shouted, "Get away from me! You are an ass! An ass!"

Dogberry replied, "Do you not suspect [respect] my job as a law-enforcement officer? Do you not suspect [respect] my age? I wish that the sexton were here so he could write down that I am an ass! But, people, remember that I am an ass. Although it is not written down, do not forget that I am an ass."

Dogberry wanted Conrade to be punished for calling him an ass, and so he wanted an official record of the name-calling.

He said to Conrade, "You villain, you are full of piety [impiety], as shall be proved upon you by good witnesses. I am a wise [foolish] fellow, and, which is more, I am a law-enforcement officer, and, which is more, I am the head of a household, and, which is more, I am as pretty a piece of flesh as any is in Messina, and I am one who knows the law [does not know the law], damn you. And I am a rich enough fellow, damn you; and I am a fellow who has suffered financial losses, and I am one who owns two gowns and has many handsome things around him. Bring him away. Oh, I wish that the sexton had written down that I am an ass!"

# CHAPTER 5

## — 5.1 —

Leonato and Antonio, his older brother, were on the street in front of Leonato's house.

"If you go on ranting and raging like this, you will kill yourself," Antonio said. "It is not wise to add to your own grief."

"Please, do not give me advice," Leonato replied. "Advice falls on my ears the way that water pours into a sieve. Neither accomplishes anything, so do not give me advice. Let no one try to comfort me except someone who has suffered what I have suffered. Bring me a father who has loved his child as much as I loved Hero. Let his joy in his child be overwhelmed by sorrow like my joy has been, and let him speak to me about patiently enduring my sorrow. Measure that father's sorrow by the length and breadth of my sorrow, and see whether his sorrow equals my sorrow and his grief equals my grief in every way — in every lineament, branch, shape, and form. If it does, then if that father will smile and stroke his beard, tell sorrow to get lost, cry 'Keep going!' instead of groaning, cure grief with proverbs, make misfortune forget itself with advice from scholars who read philosophical books, then bring that father to me. From him I will learn how to patiently endure my sorrow. But no such father exists.

"Antonio, men can give advice and speak comforting words to a man who suffers a grief that they themselves do not feel; but if they themselves feel that same grief, then their advice turns into suffering. When men do not feel grief, then they think that they can conquer rage with precepts and little life lessons. When men do not feel grief, then they think that they can tie up strong madness with a silken thread. When men do not feel grief, then they think that they can charm away aches with mere breath and charm away agony with mere words. So they think.

"All men think that it is their duty to speak about patiently enduring sorrow to those who writhe under a heavy load of sorrow. However, no man has the ability or power to be so moral when he himself is enduring the same heavy load of sorrow. Therefore, do not give me advice. My griefs cry louder than words of advice."

"Men who think and feel as you do cannot be distinguished from children," Antonio replied.

"Be quiet, please," Leonato said. "I will be flesh and blood. No philosopher has ever been able to patiently endure a toothache, even if the philosopher has written in the style of gods who do not suffer as humans do and even if the philosopher has scoffed at bad luck and suffering."

"You are suffering, but you ought not to bear all the suffering by yourself," Antonio said. "Make those men who have offended you suffer, too."

"Now you are speaking intelligently," Leonato said. "I will do that. My soul tells me now that Hero has been slandered, and I intend that Claudio shall know that, as shall Don Pedro and everyone else who thus dishonors her."

Antonio looked up and said, "Here come Don Pedro and Claudio hurrying this way."

Don Pedro and Claudio walked over to Leonato and Antonio.

Don Pedro said, "Good day."

Claudio said, "Good day to both of you."

"We are in a hurry, Leonato," Don Pedro said.

"A hurry!" Leonato said. "Well, fare you well, my lord. Are you so hasty now that my daughter is dead? Don't you want to speak to me?"

He added, sarcastically, "It doesn't matter, I suppose — to you."

Don Pedro said, "Do not quarrel with us, good old man."

Antonio said, "If Leonato could make things right by quarreling, some of the men here would lie low in their graves."

Claudio asked, "Who has done wrong to Leonato?"

"You have wronged me, Claudio," Leonato replied. "You are a liar."

Claudio's hand rested on the hilt of his sword.

Leonato pointed to Claudio's hand and said, "If you want me to be afraid, you will not accomplish that by putting your hand on your sword. I am not afraid."

"Curse my hand if it should give an old man a reason to be afraid," Claudio said. "I swear that I had no intention of drawing my sword."

"Tut, man," Leonato said. "Do not scorn or make jokes about me. I do not speak like a dotard or a fool. I do not brag about what I did when I was young, and I do not brag about what I would do if I were not old. I am telling you to your face, Claudio, that you have so wronged my innocent child and me that

I am forced to put aside my old man's respectability and, with the grey hairs and the bruises that result from living so many days, I challenge you to a duel. I say to you that you have lied about my innocent child. Your slander has gone through and through her heart, and she lies buried with her ancestors. She lies in a tomb where never scandal has slept, except this scandal of hers — scandal that is the result of your villainy and lies!"

"My villainy?" Claudio said.

"Your villainy, Claudio," Leonato said. "It is your villainy."

Don Pedro said, "You are wrong, old man."

Leonato replied, "My lord, I will prove the truth of what I say on his body, if he dares to fight me, despite his elegant fencing and his recent battle experience, his youth, and his manliness."

"No," Claudio said. "I will not fight you!"

"Do you think that you can ignore me?" Leonato said. "You have killed my daughter. If you kill me, boy, you shall kill a man."

"He shall kill two of us, and we are men indeed," Antonio said. "But that does not matter. Let Claudio kill one of us first, and then he can boast about it. Win me and wear me: Let him conquer me, and then he can boast. Let Claudio answer my challenge to him."

He said to Claudio, "Come, follow me, boy. Come, Sir Boy, and follow me. Sir Boy, I will whip you despite your fancy fencing. I am a gentleman, and I swear that I will kill you."

Leonato began, "Brother —"

"Be quiet," Antonio said. "God knows that I loved my niece, and she is dead. She was slandered to death by villains who are as eager to fight a man in a duel as I am to pick up a poisonous snake by its tongue. Who are these slanderers? Boys, mimics, braggarts, knaves, milksops!"

"Brother Antonio —"

"Be quiet. What, man! I know these slanderers. I know what kind of men they are. I know what they are made of and what they weigh down to the last gram. They are scuffling, insolent and bullying, fashion-mongering boys. They lie and cheat and insult, and they deprave and slander. They dress and behave like buffoons and look repulsive. They speak half a dozen dangerous words about how they might hurt their enemies if they dared to, and they don't dare to."

"But, brother Antonio —"

"Brother, be quiet. I know what I am doing. Do not meddle in this. Let me deal with it."

Don Pedro said, "Gentlemen, we will not stay here and disturb your peace of mind any longer. I am sorry that your daughter died, but, on my honor, I swear that she was charged with nothing but what was fully proven to be true."

Leonato began, "My lord —"

Don Pedro, who had more power than Leonato, said sharply, "I will not listen to you."

Leonato said, "No? Come, Antonio; let us leave."

Leonato then said to Don Pedro, "I will be heard!"

"And he shall," Antonio said, "or some of us here will hurt because of it."

Leonato and Antonio exited.

Benedick walked toward Don Pedro and Claudio.

Don Pedro said to Claudio, "Look, here comes the man we were looking for."

Claudio said to Benedick, "What's up?"

Benedick ignored Claudio and said to Don Pedro, "Good day, my lord."

"Welcome, Benedick," Don Pedro said. "You have almost come in time to stop what was almost a fight."

Claudio said, "Two old men without teeth wanted to bite off our noses."

"They were Leonato and his brother," Don Pedro said. "What do you think about that? Had we fought, I think that we would have been too young and strong for them."

"An unfair fight has no true valor," Benedick said. "I came looking for both of you."

"We have been everywhere looking for you," Claudio said. "We are very sad and would like to have our sadness beaten away. Will you use your wit to make us happy?"

"It is in my scabbard," Benedick said. "Shall I draw it?"

"Do you wear your wit by your side?" Don Pedro said.

"No one wears their wit by their side," Claudio said, "although some people have been out of their wits. Please draw your wit, just as minstrels draw their bows across their musical instruments, and entertain us."

"To be honest, Benedick looks pale," Don Pedro said. "Are you ill, Benedick, or are you angry?"

"Care may have killed the cat," Claudio said, "but you are strong enough to kill care."

"Sir, I shall defeat you in a battle of wits even if you charge against me at full gallop," Benedick said. "Please choose a subject to talk about other than wit."

"You need another lance to joust with," Claudio said. "Your lance has been broken across the middle. You have not directly hit your opponent."

"Benedick is growing paler and paler," Don Pedro said. "I think that he is indeed angry."

"If he is, he knows what he can do about it," Claudio said. "His anger is his problem."

"Can I talk to you privately?" Benedick asked Claudio.

"God forbid that you want to challenge me to a duel!" Claudio said.

Benedick said quietly to Claudio, "You are a villain. I am not joking, and I will prove in a duel that you are a villain. I challenge you however you like. We can use whatever weapons you like, and we will duel whenever you like. Accept my challenge, or I will make it known that you are a coward. You have killed a sweet lady, and you shall pay for her death. What is your answer to my challenge?"

"I accept your challenge," Claudio said, "and I plan to enjoy myself."

Don Pedro did not quite hear what Benedick and Claudio had said.

Don Pedro said, "Enjoy yourself? At what? A feast?"

Claudio said, "Benedick has invited me to a feast of a calf's head and a capon: a castrated cock. I have every intention of carving the capon — if I don't carve it, say that my knife is worthless. I think that I will see a woodcock at the feast, too."

Claudio thought, *Calves, capons, and woodcocks are all notorious for their stupidity.*

Benedick replied, "Sir, your wit ambles; it goes very slowly."

Don Pedro said, "Let me tell you how Beatrice praised your wit the other day, Benedick.

"I said that you had a fine wit.

"Beatrice said, 'True, a fine little wit.'

"'No,' I said. 'He has a great wit.'

"'Right,' Beatrice said. 'A great big coarse wit.'

"'No,' I said. 'A good wit.'

"'That is exactly right,' Beatrice said. 'It is so weak that it hurts nobody.'

"'No,' I said. 'The gentleman is wise.'

"'That is certain,' Beatrice said. 'He is a wiseass.'

"'No,' I said. 'He can speak in foreign tongues.'

"'I can believe that,' Beatrice said. 'Benedick swore one thing to me on Monday night, which he forswore on Tuesday morning. He has a double tongue; he has two tongues.'

"For an entire hour, she criticized you and turned all your virtues into vices, yet at last she concluded, with a sigh, that you are the handsomest man in Italy."

"And then she cried a lot and said that she did not care," Claudio said.

"Yes, she did," Don Pedro said, "but yet, for all that, she said that if she did not hate him deadly, she would love him dearly. Hero, the old man's daughter, told us all this."

"She did say all this," Claudio said, "and God saw Benedick when he was hiding in the garden the way that he saw Adam after Adam had hidden himself after sinning."

"When shall we set the savage bull's horns on the sensible Benedick's head?" Don Pedro asked.

"Yes, and when shall we put a sign on him that says, 'Here is Benedick the married man'?" Claudio said.

Don Pedro and Claudio were making inappropriate jokes about an angry man. They were now angry at Benedick, whom they had recently considered to be their friend.

Benedick said to Claudio, "Fare you well, boy. You know what I think about you. I will leave you now to your old woman's chattering: You break jests as braggarts do their blades, which God be thanked, hurt not. Braggarts will hack their own swords in private, and then say in public that their swords were damaged in battle."

Benedick said to Don Pedro, "My lord, for your many courtesies I thank you, but I must discontinue your company and leave your service. Your brother Don John the bastard has fled from Messina. You, Claudio, and Don John have among you killed a sweet and innocent lady. As for my Lord Lackbeard —

Claudio — there, he and I shall meet in a duel, and until then, peace be with him."

Benedick left the two men, his former friends.

Don Pedro said to Claudio, "He is in earnest. He wants to fight you."

"He is in most profound earnest, and, I promise you, he wants to fight me because he loves Beatrice."

"And he has challenged you," Don Pedro said.

"Most sincerely."

"What a pretty thing a man is when he goes about in his jacket and pants, but wears no cloak so that he can duel, and leaves behind at home his intelligence!" Don Pedro said.

"A man who makes a challenge seems to be a hero to a fool, but actually the fool is the wiser man," Claudio said.

"But wait a minute," Don Pedro said. "Let me be serious. Didn't Benedick say that Don John, my bastard brother, has fled? He must have fled for a reason that is sure to be bad news for me."

Dogberry, Verges, and the watchmen arrived. With them were Borachio and Conrade — the prisoners' hands were bound.

Dogberry said to Borachio, "Come along. If justice cannot tame and punish you, she shall never weigh more reasons in her balance. You have been a cursing hypocrite at least once, and you must be dealt with."

"What is going on?" Don Pedro said. "Two of my brother's men have been bound by this city's law-enforcement officers. Borachio is one of my brother's men who have been bound."

"Ask what is their offense, my lord," Claudio said.

"Officers, what offence have these men done?" Don Pedro asked.

Dogberry answered, "Indeed, sir, they have committed false report; moreover, they have spoken untruths; secondarily, they are slanderers; sixth and lastly, they have lied about a lady; thirdly, they have verified unjust things; and, to conclude, they are lying knaves."

Amused by Dogberry's answer, Don Pedro replied, "First, I ask you what they have done; thirdly, I ask you what is their offence; sixth and lastly, I ask you why they are committed; and, to conclude, I ask you what you lay to their charge."

"That is a good reply, and it is in his own style," Claudio said to Don Pedro. "Truly, he has said one thing in six different ways."

Don Pedro asked the prisoners, "Who have you offended, masters, that your hands are thus bound and you must answer to these law-enforcement officers? This learned constable is too cunning for me to understand. What is your offence?"

Borachio had repented his sin. He had been willing to be somewhat evil, but he had not intended to help cause the death of a lady. That was too evil for him.

Borachio said to Don Pedro, "Sweet Prince, let me answer you immediately. Hear my confession, and then let Count Claudio kill me. I have deceived your own eyes. What wise men could not uncover, these shallow fools have brought to light. The watchmen during the night overheard me confessing to this man, Conrade, how Don John your brother instigated me to slander the Lady Hero. They overheard me tell how you were brought to Leonato's garden and saw me court Margaret, who was wearing some of Hero's clothing. Count Claudio disgraced Hero when he was supposed to marry her. My confession of my villainy they have upon record. I would rather pay for my villainy with my death than recount again what I have done. The lady Hero is dead because of the false accusation of unchasteness that Don John and I have engineered, and to be short, I want nothing but the reward of a villain — I want to be justly punished for my crime."

"Doesn't this speech make your blood run cold?" Don Pedro said to Claudio.

"This speech is like poison to me," Claudio said.

"Did Don John tempt you to do all this?" Don Pedro asked Borachio.

"Yes, and he paid me richly for doing it."

"Don John delights in treachery," Don Pedro said, "and he has fled to escape being punished for this villainy."

"Sweet Hero!" Claudio said. "Now when I think of you, I remember you the way you appeared when I first loved you."

Dogberry said, "Come, bring away the plaintiffs [defendants]. By this time, the sexton has reformed [informed] Signior Leonato about what we have learned, and, masters, do not forget to specify, when you have time and are in the right place, that I am an ass."

Verges said, "Here comes master Signior Leonato, and the sexton, too."

Leonato, Antonio, and the sexton walked over to the others.

Leonato said, "Which man is the villain? Let me see his eyes so that, when I see another man like him, I may avoid him. Which of these men is he?"

"If you want to see the man who wronged you," Borachio said, "look at me."

"Are you the slave and scoundrel who with your lying breath has killed my innocent child?"

"Yes, I alone did that," Borachio said.

"That is not true, villain," Leonato replied. "You did not kill my daughter by yourself. Here stand a pair of 'honorable' men who helped kill my daughter. A third guilty man has fled."

He said sarcastically to Don Pedro and Claudio, "I thank you, sirs, for my daughter's death. Record it with your other high and worthy deeds. It was brave of you to do so; think well of yourselves when you think of your deed."

When someone does wrong, even unintentionally, it is often best to admit the fact and accept the punishment.

Claudio said to Leonato, "I do not know how to ask for your forgiveness, yet I must speak up and ask for it. Choose your revenge yourself; impose on me whatever penance you think is suitable to punish my sin, although I sinned not on purpose but by mistake."

Don Pedro said, "I also sinned by mistake. And yet, to satisfy this good old man, Leonato, I am willing to bend under any heavy weight that he wishes to place on me."

"I cannot order you to make my daughter live again," Leonato said. "That is impossible, but I ask you both to inform the people in Messina here that she was innocent and a virgin when she died. Claudio, if your love can labor in creation despite your sadness, then write an epitaph for Hero and hang it on a wall in her tomb and sing it to her bones. Sing it tonight, and tomorrow morning come to my house. Because Hero is dead, you cannot be my son-in-law, but you can yet be my nephew. My brother has a daughter who is almost the twin — almost an exact copy — of my daughter who is dead. My brother's daughter is the sole heir to both of us. Marry my brother's daughter, and that will end the enmity between us."

"Oh, noble sir, your great kindness wrings tears from me! I embrace your offer, and I put my future in your hands."

"I will expect you to come to my house tomorrow morning to be married," Leonato said. "For tonight I take my leave of you. This wicked man shall be brought face to face with Margaret, whom I believe was part of this evil plot and bribed to participate in it by Don John."

"I swear on my soul that Margaret is innocent," Borachio said. "She did not know about the plot when I spoke to her outside Hero's bedroom window. Margaret has always been just and virtuous in everything."

Dogberry said, "Moreover, sir, here is something that has not been written down in white and black. This plaintiff [defendant] here, the offender, did call me an ass. I ask you to let that be remembered in his punishment. Also, the watchmen heard these men talk about a man named De Formed. They said that he wears a key in his ear and has a lock hanging by it, and he borrows money in God's name, something that he has done for so long and never paid the money back that now men grow hard-hearted and will lend nothing for God's sake. Please, examine De Formed about that charge."

"I thank you for your care and honest pains," Leonato replied.

"Your worship speaks like a most thankful and reverend youth [old man], and I praise God for you," Dogberry replied.

Handing Dogberry some money, Leonato said, "Here is something for your good work."

"God save the foundation!" Dogberry said, using a sentence spoken by professional beggars.

"You may go now," Leonato said. "I will take care of your prisoners. Thank you."

"I leave an arrant knave with your worship," Dogberry said, "and I beg your worship to correct yourself [punish Borachio] to serve as an example to others. God keep your worship! I wish your worship well! God restore you to health! I humbly give you leave to depart [I will now humbly depart]; and if a merry meeting may be wished, may God prohibit [permit] it! Let's go, Verges."

Dogberry and Verges exited.

Leonato said to Don Pedro and Count Claudio, "Until tomorrow morning, lords, farewell."

"As we promised, we will see you tomorrow morning," Don Pedro said.

"Tonight I will go to Hero's tomb to mourn her," Claudio said.

Leonato said to the watchmen, "Bring the prisoners. We will talk to Margaret and find out how she became acquainted with this scoundrel."

— 5.2 —

In Leonato's garden, Benedick and Margaret talked.

"Please, sweet Mistress Margaret, earn my thanks by asking Beatrice to come and talk to me."

"If I do, will you then write me a sonnet in praise of my beauty?"

"Yes," Benedick said. "I will write it in so high a style, Margaret, that no man living shall exceed its eloquence. It will be like a high stile that no man can climb and come over it. Truly, Margaret, you deserve it."

"I deserve to have no man come over me!" Margaret said. "In that case, I will always sleep downstairs in the servants' quarters. I will never have a husband who will be over me in our bed in our own household and cum."

"Your wit is as quick as a greyhound's mouth; it catches everything and makes a joke out of it."

"Your wit is as blunt as a fencer's foils, which hit, but do not hurt."

"I have a very manly wit, Margaret," Benedick said. "It will not hurt a woman, and so please ask Beatrice to come and talk to me. I give up in this battle of wits. To show that I give up, I will give you my fencing buckler — my small, round shield."

"Give us women swords," Margaret said. "We have bucklers to press against your swords."

Benedick was familiar with Margaret's bawdy sense of humor. When conversing with Margaret, Benedick understood that swords are phalluses and that bucklers are women's crotches.

Benedick said, "Margaret, each buckler has a hole in which a pike is inserted — it is screwed in. Screwing is a dangerous pastime for virgins."

"I will ask Beatrice to come to you," Margaret said. "I think that she has legs."

"And because she has legs, she will come," Benedick said, thinking, *I am sure that Margaret will think that I said, "And because she has legs, she will cum."*

Margaret exited.

Benedick began to sing to himself a song about a sad lover hoping for attention from the woman he loved:

*"The god of love,*

"*Who sits above,*
"*And knows me, and knows me,*
"*How pitiful I deserve —*

"I am a poor singer, but I am a good lover. Leander was a good swimmer who swam across the Hellespont to see the woman he loved. Troilus was the first employer of panders to help him to see the woman he loved. These two men and a whole book full of these old-time ladies' men who were familiar with the carpeted floor of women's quarters, all of whose names fit smoothly in the even sound of a poem of blank verse, why, they were never so truly turned topsy-turvy in love as I am. But although that is true, I cannot show my love in rhyme, although I have tried. I can find no rhyme for 'lady' but 'baby.' That is an innocent and silly rhyme for an innocent and silly baby. I can find no rhyme for 'scorn' but 'horn.' That is a hard rhyme for a hard horn. I can find no rhyme for 'school' but 'fool.' That is a babbling rhyme. These are very ominous words to put at the end of lines of poetry: baby … horn … fool. They would fit, however, for a poem about a foolish cuckold whose wife gives birth to another man's baby. Well, I was not born under a rhyming planet and so I receive no help from astrology. I am no poet, and I cannot woo a lady with flowery language."

Beatrice appeared, and Benedick said to her, "Sweet Beatrice, have you come because I asked Margaret to ask you to come? If so, I am delighted."

"Yes, I have come because you bid me to come, and I will leave when you bid me to leave, but the word 'bid' also means order, and I will leave if you begin to order me around."

"Please stay until then!"

"Until … then? You have said the word 'then,' and so I should say 'fare you well' and leave," Beatrice said. "However, before I go, tell me what I came here to learn: What has happened between you and Claudio?"

"So far, we have only exchanged foul words, and with that I will kiss you."

"Is that all? Foul words are only foul wind, and foul wind is only foul breath, and foul breath stinks. You have had foul words in your mouth, and so your breath must stink; therefore, I will depart unkissed."

"Your wit is strong — so strong that it can frighten my words and so change their meaning," Benedick said. "But I must tell you plainly that I have challenged Claudio. Either I will shortly hear from him about where and when we shall fight, or I will announce publicly that he is a coward. But now let me ask you, please, this question: Because of which of my bad character traits did you first fall in love with me?"

"I fell in love with you because of all of your bad character traits," Beatrice said. "Your bad character traits are so well maintained in a state of evil that they will not admit any good character traits to intermingle with them. But now let me ask you, please, this question: Because of which of my good character traits did you first fall in love with me? For which one did you first suffer love for me?"

"'Suffer love!' That is a good expression!" Benedick said. "I do suffer love indeed, because I love you against my will."

"You love me in spite of your heart," Beatrice said. "Alas, poor heart! If you spite your poor heart for my sake, I will spite it for yours; I will never love that which my friend hates."

"You and I are too wise and witty to woo peacefully."

"Your words cannot be correct," Beatrice said. "You say that you are wise, but not one wise man out of twenty will praise himself by saying that he is wise."

"The proverb 'A wise man will not praise himself' is very old, Beatrice. It comes from the good old days when neighbors spoke well of other people. These days are different. These days, if a man does not erect his own tomb before he dies, he shall live no longer in memory than the time it takes the bell to ring and the widow to weep."

"And how long is that, do you think?"

"That is an interesting question," Benedick said. "The funeral bell will ring for an hour, and the widow will weep for fifteen minutes. Therefore, it is most expedient for a wise man, if his conscience, which can be like a gnawing worm, finds no reason against it, to be the trumpet of his own virtues, as I am to myself. But that is enough of my praising myself, although I myself bear witness that I am praiseworthy. Now tell me, how is Hero, your cousin?"

"She is very ill."

"And how are you?"

"Very ill, too."

"Serve God, love me, and get better," Benedick said. "Now I should leave you because I see someone running here."

Ursula ran up to Beatrice and said, "Madam, you must go to your uncle. All kinds of exciting things are going on at home. It has been proven that my Lady

Hero has been falsely accused of being unchaste, Don Pedro and Claudio have been greatly deceived, and Don John, who has fled, is the instigator of all this evil. Will you go home immediately?"

"Will you go with us to hear this news, Benedick?" Beatrice asked.

"I will live in your heart, die in your lap from an orgasm, and be buried in your eyes when I see reflected in them my O face," Benedick said, "and moreover I will go with you to your uncle's home."

They went inside Leonato's house.

— 5.3 —

That night, Don Pedro, Claudio, some musicians, and a few attendants carrying burning torches entered the tomb in which they thought Hero was buried.

Claudio asked, "Is this the tomb of the family of Leonato?"

An attendant replied, "It is, my lord."

Claudio began to read a scroll that contained a poem that he had written about Hero:

*"Done to death by slanderous tongues*

*"Was the Hero who here lies:*

*"Death, in recompense of her wrongs,*

*"Gives her fame that never dies.*

*"So the life that died with shame*

*"Lives in death with glorious fame."*

Claudio hung the scroll containing the poem on a wall of the tomb and said, "Hang here in the tomb and praise Hero when I am silent. Now, music, play, and let us sing a solemn hymn."

Music started, and the mourners sang this song as they circled clockwise what they thought was Hero's resting place:

*"Pardon, Diana, goddess of the night,*

*"Those who slew Hero, your virgin knight;*

*"For which, with songs of woe,*

*"Round about her tomb they go.*

*"Midnight, assist our moan;*

*"Help us to sigh and groan,*

*"Heavily, heavily:*

*"Graves, yawn and yield your dead,*

*"Until all the dead have exited,*

*"Heavily, heavily."*

Claudio said to the resting place that he thought was Hero's, "Now to your bones I say good night! Yearly I will do this rite."

Don Pedro said, "Good morrow, masters; put out your torches. The wolves have hunted all night — look, the gentle day, brought to us by the wheels

92

of Phoebus Apollo's Sun-chariot, dapples the drowsy East with spots of grey. Thanks to you all, and leave us. Fare you well."

Claudio said goodbye to the other mourners: "Good morning, masters. Each of you must go his separate way."

"Come, Claudio, let us leave us here," Don Pedro said. "We need to change out of our mourning clothing and put on clothing suitable for a wedding. Then we will go to Leonato's house."

"May Hymen, the god of marriage, now give us a luckier result than this one for which we have this night mourned."

Leonato, Antonio, Benedick, Beatrice, Margaret, Ursula, Friar Francis, and Hero were together in a room in Leonato's house.

Friar Francis said, "Didn't I tell you that Hero was innocent?"

"Yes, you did," Leonato admitted. "Don Pedro and Claudio are also innocent, although they mistakenly accused Hero of not being a virgin. But Margaret bears some little fault for all this, although her fault was unintentional, as we have learned from our investigation."

Antonio said, "I am glad that things have turned out so well."

"And so am I," Benedick said, "or else I would have to fight Claudio in a duel, as I promised Beatrice I would do."

Leonato said, "Well, daughter, and all of you gentlewomen, go into a room by yourselves, and when I send for you, come here wearing masks."

Hero, Beatrice, Margaret, and Ursula left the room.

Leonato said, "Don Pedro and Claudio promised to visit me right about now. You know what to do, brother Antonio. You must pretend to be the father of your brother's daughter, Hero, and give her to young Claudio."

"I will do so with a straight face," Antonio said.

Benedick said, "Friar Francis, I must ask for your help."

"To do what, Signior Benedick?"

"To bind me, or to undo me: one of them," Benedick said. "Either I will be married today to the woman I love, or I will be undone in the sense of being ruined, although I hope to be undone — released — from my pose of being a misogynist."

He then said, "Good Signior Leonato, it is true that Beatrice, your niece, regards me with an eye of favor. She loves me."

"My daughter, Hero, lent her that eye," Leonato said, thinking of how Hero and Margaret had tricked Beatrice into believing that Benedick loved her.

"And I do with an eye of love requite her," Benedick said. "I love her."

"And you received your eye from me, Don Pedro, and Claudio," Leonato said, thinking of how the three men, including himself, had tricked Benedick into believing that Beatrice loved him. "But what do you want?"

Benedick, who was puzzled by Leonato's comments about eyes, said, "Your answers to me, sir, are enigmatic. But what my will wants is your good will. I want to stand with Beatrice beside me today as we are joined in marriage. And, good friar, I need you to perform that marriage."

"I like what you want," Leonato said. "I give you my blessing. You may marry Beatrice."

"And you will receive my help," Friar Francis said. "I will perform the wedding."

He added, "Here come Don Pedro and Count Claudio."

A few people accompanied Don Pedro and Claudio.

Don Pedro said, "Good morning to all in this fair assembly."

"Good morning, Don Pedro," Leonato said. "Good morning, Claudio. We have been waiting for you. Claudio, are you still resolved to marry my brother's daughter today?"

"I am still resolved," Claudio said. "I will marry her even if she is darkly suntanned like a peasant woman."

Leonato said, "Bring her here, brother Antonio. The friar is ready to perform the wedding."

Antonio left to get Hero, Beatrice, Margaret, and Ursula.

Don Pedro looked at Benedick, who was a little worried about being teased by Don Pedro and Claudio when they discovered that he would marry Beatrice.

Don Pedro said to Benedick, with whom he wanted to be again on good — and joking — terms, "Good morning, Benedick. Why, what is the matter? You have a February face that is full of frost, storm, and cloudiness."

Benedick was worried — he had not actually asked Beatrice to marry him. If she rejected his proposal in public ...

Claudio, who also wanted to be again on good — and joking — terms with Benedick, said, "I think that Benedick is thinking about the savage bull that was tamed to bear the yoke. Tut, fear not, Benedick. If you are ever tamed, we will tip your horns with gold to glorify your cuckoldry. All of Europe shall rejoice, like Europa once rejoiced when the lusty god Jupiter turned himself into a bull and carried her away to make love to her."

Worried about whether Beatrice would accept his proposal of marriage, Benedick replied, "When Jupiter was a bull, he had an amiable lowing sound. Another strange bull jumped on your father's cow, and made a calf in that same noble deed that Jupiter performed on Europa. That calf was very similar to you — you have that calf's bleat."

Claudio joked, "I'll get you for that insult, but later. Right now, I have something else I need to do."

Antonio returned. With him were Hero, Beatrice, Margaret, and Ursula, all of whom were wearing masks.

Claudio asked, "Which lady shall be mine?"

Antonio took Hero by the hand and led her to Claudio, saying, "This lady is she, and I do give her to you."

"Why, then she is mine," Claudio said. "Sweet lady, let me see your face."

"No, you shall not," Leonato said, "not until you take her hand before this friar and swear to marry her."

Claudio said to the masked Hero, whom he did not recognize, "Give me your hand. Before this holy friar, I swear that I will be your husband, if you are willing to take me."

Hero replied, "When I lived, I was your other wife."

She took off her mask and said, "And when you loved me, you were my other husband."

Claudio was amazed: "Another Hero!"

"Nothing is more certain than that I am Hero," she replied. "One Hero died, defiled and slandered, but I live, and as surely as I live, I am a virgin."

"This is the former Hero!" Don Pedro said, "This is the Hero who was dead!"

"Hero died, my lord, only while her slander lived," Leonato said. "This is the one and only Hero."

"All this amazement I can explain," Friar Francis said, "after the holy rites of marriage are over. Then I will tell you in detail of beautiful Hero's 'death.' In the meantime, ignore your wonder, and let us go immediately to the chapel."

"Just a minute, Friar Francis," Benedick said. "Which masked lady is Beatrice?"

Beatrice took off her mask and said, "I answer to that name. What do you want?"

"Do you love me?" Benedick asked.

Declaring one's love in private is much easier than declaring one's love in public, especially when you are surrounded by friends who will laugh at you because you have so often spoken against love and marriage. Besides, the guy is supposed to be the first one to say that he is in love — and the first one to say that he will take someone as a spouse.

Beatrice replied, "Why, no — no more than is reasonable."

"Why, then your uncle and Don Pedro and Claudio have been deceived; they swore you loved me," Benedick said.

Beatrice asked, "Do you love me?"

"Indeed, I love you — no more than is reasonable," Benedick said.

"Why, then Hero, Margaret, and Ursula have been deceived; they swore you loved me," Beatrice said.

"Leonato and Don Pedro and Claudio swore that you were almost sick because you loved me so much."

"Hero and Margaret and Ursula swore that you were almost dead because you loved me so much."

"They were mistaken," Benedick said. "Then you do not love me?"

Beatrice said, "No, truly, but I love you as a friend."

The two lovers needed help.

Leonato said, "Come, Beatrice, I am sure that you love Benedick."

Claudio said, "I swear that Benedick loves Beatrice. I have in my hand a piece of paper on which he has written a poem of his own invention. It is a badly written love poem, and in it he says that he loves Beatrice."

Hero said, "And I have in my hand a piece of paper that I have stolen from Beatrice's pocket. I recognize her writing, and in this letter she says that she loves Benedick."

Benedick said, "We needed a miracle, and we have received one. Here is evidence from our hands that reveal what is our hearts. Beatrice, I will take you for my wife, but —" he smiled, then joked, "I want everyone to know that I am marrying you because I pity you for loving me so much."

Beatrice replied, "I accept your offer of marriage, but —" she smiled, then joked, "I want everyone to know that I am marrying you only after quite a lot of persuasion and in part because I want to save your life, for I was told that you were dying because of your love for me."

"Be silent!" Benedick said. "I will stop your mouth."

They kissed.

"How is Benedick the soon-to-be-married man doing?" Don Pedro asked.

"I will tell you what, Don Pedro," Benedick replied, relieved that his proposal of marriage had been accepted. "An entire company of jokers cannot mock me out of my happy state of mind. Do you think that I worry about being mocked in a satire or an epigram? No. If a man worries about being beaten by brains, he will do nothing that would make him a target, such as wearing fancy clothing. In brief, since I do intend to marry — today, in fact — I will think nothing about whatever the world can say against me. Don't bother to mock me because of what I have said against marriage. Mankind is a giddy and inconstant thing, and this is the way that I have changed, and I like it."

He added, "Claudio, I would have defeated you in our duel, but since we are going to be related by our marriages, I will let you live unbruised so that you can love one of my new family members: Hero."

"I wish that you would have refused to marry Beatrice," Claudio said. "That way, I could have beaten you and forced you to marry her. Then you could be a double-dealer — an unfaithful husband. Come to think of it, you are likely to be a double-dealer unless Beatrice keeps a close eye on you."

"Come, come, we are friends," Benedick said. "Let us dance before we are married, so that we may lighten our own hearts — and our wives' heels."

Leonato said, "Light heels! Have the wedding first, and then you can do your dancing in bed afterwards with your wives' heels high in the air."

"We will do that kind of dancing later, just as you wish," Benedick said. "But now let us have a public kind of dancing. Therefore, musicians, play music. Don Pedro, you seem sad. Get yourself a wife; get yourself a wife. No staff is more honorable than one tipped with horn."

A messenger entered the room and said to Don Pedro, "My lord, your brother, Don John, has been captured as he fled. Armed men are bringing him back to Messina."

"Don't worry about Don John until tomorrow," Benedick said to Don Pedro. "I will think up some suitable and notable punishments for him."

He shouted, "Strike up some music, pipers."

Everyone danced.

# APPENDIX A: ABOUT THE AUTHOR

It was a dark and stormy night. Suddenly a cry rang out, and on a hot summer night in 1954, Josephine, wife of Carl Bruce, gave birth to a boy — me. Unfortunately, this young married couple allowed Reuben Saturday, Josephine's brother, to name their first-born. Reuben, aka "The Joker," decided that Bruce was a nice name, so he decided to name me Bruce Bruce. I have gone by my middle name — David — ever since.

Being named Bruce David Bruce hasn't been all bad. Bank tellers remember me very quickly, so I don't often have to show an ID. It can be fun in charades, also. When I was a counselor as a teenager at Camp Echoing Hills in Warsaw, Ohio, a fellow counselor gave the signs for "sounds like" and "two words," then she pointed to a bruise on her leg twice. Bruise Bruise? Oh yeah, Bruce Bruce is the answer!

Uncle Reuben, by the way, gave me a haircut when I was in kindergarten. He cut my hair short and shaved a small bald spot on the back of my head. My mother wouldn't let me go to school until the bald spot grew out again.

Of all my brothers and sisters (six in all), I am the only transplant to Athens, Ohio. I was born in Newark, Ohio, and have lived all around Southeastern Ohio. However, I moved to Athens to go to Ohio University and have never left.

At Ohio U, I never could make up my mind whether to major in English or Philosophy, so I got a bachelor's degree with a double major in both areas, then I added a Master of Arts degree in English and a Master of Arts degree in Philosophy. Yes, I have my MAMA degree.

Currently, and for a long time to come (I eat fruits and veggies), I am spending my retirement writing books such as *Nadia Comaneci: Perfect 10*, *The Funniest People in Dance*, *Homer's* Iliad: *A Retelling in Prose*, and *William Shakespeare's* Othello: *A Retelling in Prose*.

By the way, my sister Brenda Kennedy writes romances such as *A New Beginning* and *Shattered Dreams*.

# APPENDIX B: SOME BOOKS BY DAVID BRUCE

**Retellings of a Classic Work of Literature**

Arden of Faversham: *A Retelling*

*Ben Jonson's* The Alchemist: *A Retelling*

*Ben Jonson's* The Arraignment, or Poetaster: *A Retelling*

*Ben Jonson's* Bartholomew Fair: *A Retelling*

*Ben Jonson's* The Case is Altered: *A Retelling*

*Ben Jonson's* Catiline's Conspiracy: *A Retelling*

*Ben Jonson's* The Devil is an Ass: *A Retelling*

*Ben Jonson's* Epicene: *A Retelling*

*Ben Jonson's* Every Man in His Humor: *A Retelling*

*Ben Jonson's* Every Man Out of His Humor: *A Retelling*

*Ben Jonson's* The Fountain of Self-Love, or Cynthia's Revels: *A Retelling*

*Ben Jonson's* The Magnetic Lady, or Humors Reconciled: *A Retelling*

*Ben Jonson's* The New Inn, or The Light Heart: *A Retelling*

*Ben Jonson's* Sejanus' Fall: *A Retelling*

*Ben Jonson's* The Staple of News: *A Retelling*

*Ben Jonson's* A Tale of a Tub: *A Retelling*

*Ben Jonson's* Volpone, or the Fox: *A Retelling*

*Christopher Marlowe's Complete Plays: Retellings*

*Christopher Marlowe's* Dido, Queen of Carthage: *A Retelling*

*Christopher Marlowe's* Doctor Faustus: *Retellings of the 1604 A-Text and of the 1616 B-Text*

*Christopher Marlowe's* Edward II: *A Retelling*

*Christopher Marlowe's* The Massacre at Paris: *A Retelling*

*Christopher Marlowe's* The Rich Jew of Malta: *A Retelling*

*Christopher Marlowe's* Tamburlaine, Parts 1 and 2: *Retellings*

*Dante's* Divine Comedy: *A Retelling in Prose*

*Dante's* Inferno: *A Retelling in Prose*

*Dante's* Purgatory: *A Retelling in Prose*

*Dante's* Paradise: *A Retelling in Prose*

The Famous Victories of Henry V: *A Retelling*

*From the* Iliad *to the* Odyssey: *A Retelling in Prose of Quintus of Smyrna's* Posthomerica

*George Chapman, Ben Jonson, and John Marston's* Eastward Ho! *A Retelling*

*George Peele's* The Arraignment of Paris: *A Retelling*

*George Peele's* The Battle of Alcazar: *A Retelling*

*George's Peele's* David and Bathsheba, and the Tragedy of Absalom: *A Retelling*

*George Peele's* Edward I: *A Retelling*

*George Peele's* The Old Wives' Tale: *A Retelling*

George-a-Greene: *A Retelling*

The History of King Leir: *A Retelling*

*Homer's* Iliad: *A Retelling in Prose*

*Homer's* Odyssey: *A Retelling in Prose*

*J.W. Gent.'s* The Valiant Scot: *A Retelling*

*Jason and the Argonauts: A Retelling in Prose of Apollonius of Rhodes'* Argonautica

*John Ford: Eight Plays Translated into Modern English*

*John Ford's* The Broken Heart: *A Retelling*

*John Ford's* The Fancies, Chaste and Noble: *A Retelling*

*John Ford's* The Lady's Trial: *A Retelling*

*John Ford's* The Lover's Melancholy: *A Retelling*

*John Ford's* Love's Sacrifice: *A Retelling*

*John Ford's* Perkin Warbeck: *A Retelling*

*John Ford's* The Queen: *A Retelling*

*John Ford's* 'Tis Pity She's a Whore: *A Retelling*

*John Lyly's* Campaspe: *A Retelling*

*John Lyly's* Endymion, The Man in the Moon: *A Retelling*

*John Lyly's* Galatea: *A Retelling*

*John Lyly's* Love's Metamorphosis: *A Retelling*

*John Lyly's* Midas: *A Retelling*

*John Lyly's* Mother Bombie: *A Retelling*

*John Lyly's* Sappho and Phao: *A Retelling*

*John Lyly's* The Woman in the Moon: *A Retelling*

*John Webster's* The White Devil: *A Retelling*

King Edward III: *A Retelling*

Mankind: *A Medieval Morality Play* (A Retelling)

*Margaret Cavendish's* The Unnatural Tragedy: *A Retelling*

The Merry Devil of Edmonton: *A Retelling*

The Summoning of Everyman: *A Medieval Morality Play* (A Retelling)

*Robert Greene's* Friar Bacon and Friar Bungay: *A Retelling*

The Taming of a Shrew: *A Retelling*

*Tarlton's Jests: A Retelling*

*Thomas Middleton's* A Chaste Maid in Cheapside: *A Retelling*

*Thomas Middleton's* Women Beware Women: *A Retelling*

*Thomas Middleton and Thomas Dekker's* The Roaring Girl: *A Retelling*

*Thomas Middleton and William Rowley's* The Changeling: *A Retelling*

*The Trojan War and Its Aftermath: Four Ancient Epic Poems*

*Virgil's* Aeneid: *A Retelling in Prose*

*William Shakespeare's 5 Late Romances: Retellings in Prose*

*William Shakespeare's 10 Histories: Retellings in Prose*

*William Shakespeare's 11 Tragedies: Retellings in Prose*

*William Shakespeare's 12 Comedies: Retellings in Prose*

*William Shakespeare's 38 Plays: Retellings in Prose*

*William Shakespeare's* 1 Henry IV, aka Henry IV, Part 1: *A Retelling in Prose*

*William Shakespeare's* 2 Henry IV, aka Henry IV, Part 2: *A Retelling in Prose*

*William Shakespeare's* 1 Henry VI, aka Henry VI, Part 1: *A Retelling in Prose*

*William Shakespeare's* 2 Henry VI, aka Henry VI, Part 2: *A Retelling in Prose*

*William Shakespeare's* 3 Henry VI, aka Henry VI, Part 3: *A Retelling in Prose*

*William Shakespeare's* All's Well that Ends Well: *A Retelling in Prose*

*William Shakespeare's* Antony and Cleopatra: *A Retelling in Prose*

*William Shakespeare's* As You Like It: *A Retelling in Prose*

*William Shakespeare's* The Comedy of Errors: *A Retelling in Prose*

*William Shakespeare's* Coriolanus: *A Retelling in Prose*

*William Shakespeare's* Cymbeline: *A Retelling in Prose*

*William Shakespeare's* Hamlet: *A Retelling in Prose*

*William Shakespeare's* Henry V: *A Retelling in Prose*

*William Shakespeare's* Henry VIII: *A Retelling in Prose*

*William Shakespeare's* Julius Caesar: *A Retelling in Prose*

*William Shakespeare's* King John: *A Retelling in Prose*

*William Shakespeare's* King Lear: *A Retelling in Prose*

*William Shakespeare's* Love's Labor's Lost: *A Retelling in Prose*

*William Shakespeare's* Macbeth: *A Retelling in Prose*

*William Shakespeare's* Measure for Measure: *A Retelling in Prose*

*William Shakespeare's* The Merchant of Venice: *A Retelling in Prose*

*William Shakespeare's* The Merry Wives of Windsor: *A Retelling in Prose*

*William Shakespeare's* A Midsummer Night's Dream: *A Retelling in Prose*

*William Shakespeare's* Much Ado About Nothing: *A Retelling in Prose*

*William Shakespeare's* Othello: *A Retelling in Prose*

*William Shakespeare's* Pericles, Prince of Tyre: *A Retelling in Prose*

*William Shakespeare's* Richard II: *A Retelling in Prose*

*William Shakespeare's* Richard III: *A Retelling in Prose*

*William Shakespeare's* Romeo and Juliet: *A Retelling in Prose*

*William Shakespeare's* The Taming of the Shrew: *A Retelling in Prose*

*William Shakespeare's* The Tempest: *A Retelling in Prose*

*William Shakespeare's* Timon of Athens: *A Retelling in Prose*

*William Shakespeare's* Titus Andronicus: *A Retelling in Prose*

*William Shakespeare's* Troilus and Cressida: *A Retelling in Prose*

*William Shakespeare's* Twelfth Night: *A Retelling in Prose*

*William Shakespeare's* The Two Gentlemen of Verona: *A Retelling in Prose*

*William Shakespeare's* The Two Noble Kinsmen: *A Retelling in Prose*

*William Shakespeare's* The Winter's Tale: *A Retelling in Prose*